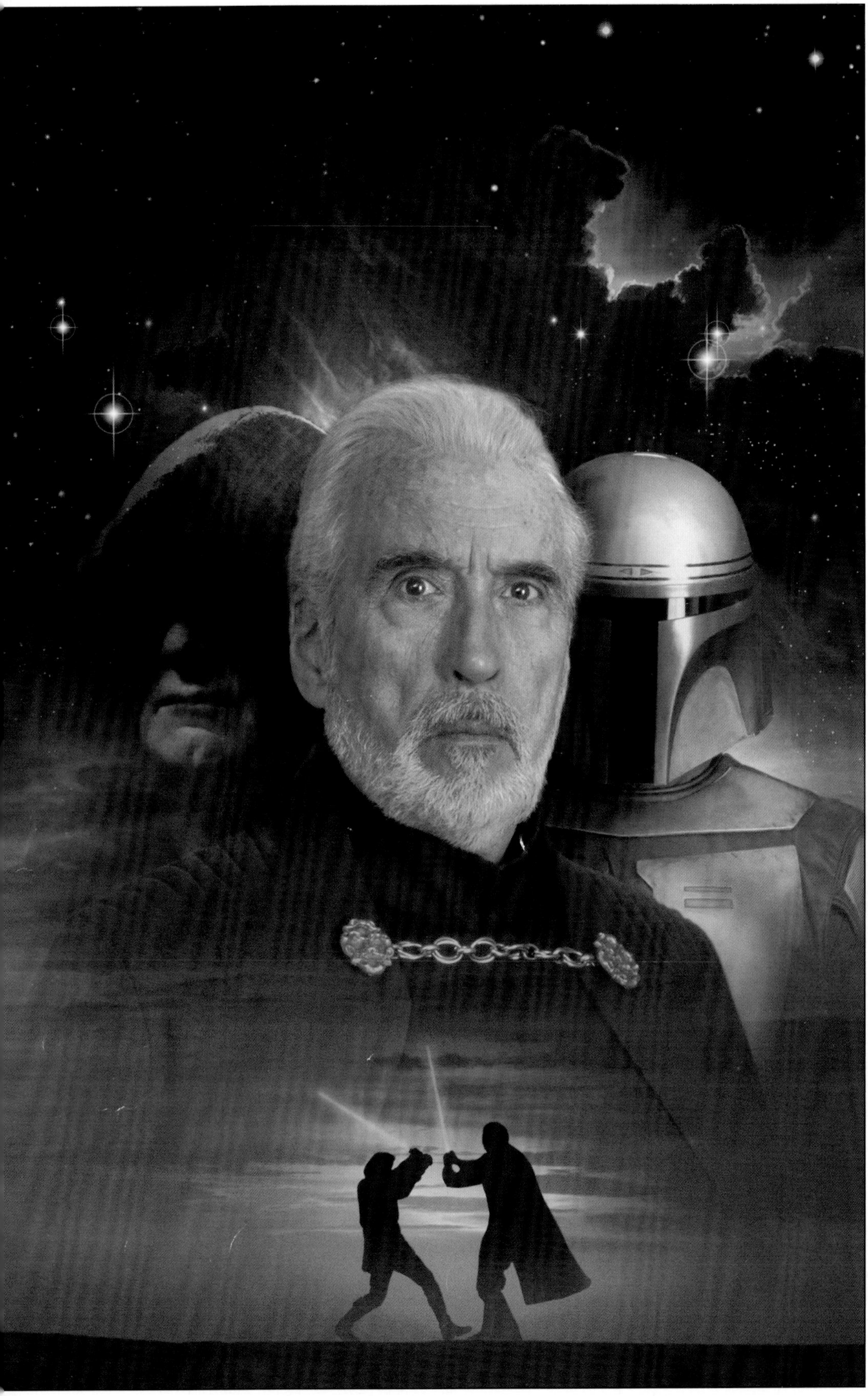

STAR WARS®

EPISODE II
ATTACK OF THE CLONES™

VOLUME TWO

ADAPTED BY
HENRY GILROY

BASED ON THE ORIGINAL STORY BY
GEORGE LUCAS

AND THE SCREENPLAY BY
GEORGE LUCAS AND
JONATHAN HALES

PENCILS
JAN DUURSEMA

INKS
RAY KRYSSING

COLORS
DAVE MCCAIG

COLOR SEPARATOR
HAROLD MACKINNON

LETTERS
STEVE DUTRO

COVER ART
TSUNEO SANDA

DARK HORSE COMICS

Spotlight

VISIT US AT
www.abdopublishing.com

Reinforced library bound edition published in 2009 by Spotlight, a division of the ABDO Group, 8000 West 78th Street, Edina, Minnesota 55439. Spotlight produces high-quality reinforced library bound editions for schools and libraries. Published by agreement with Dark Horse Comics, Inc., and Lucasfilm Ltd.

Library of Congress Cataloging-in-Publication Data

Gilroy, Henry.
Episode II : attack of the clones / story, George Lucas ; script, Henry Gilroy ; pencils, Jan Duursema ; inks, Ray Kryssing ; colors, Dave McCaig ; letters, Steve Dutro. -- Reinforced library bound ed.
    p. cm. -- (Star Wars)
ISBN 978-1-59961-612-4 (v. 1) -- ISBN 978-1-59961-613-1 (v. 2) – ISBN 978-1-59961-614-8 (v. 3) -- ISBN 978-1-59961-615-5 (v. 4)
1. Graphic novels. [1. Graphic novels.] I. Lucas, George, 1944- II. Duursema, Jan, ill. III. Kryssing, Ray. IV. McCaig, Dave. V. Dutro, Steve. VI. Star wars, Episode II, attack of the clones (Motion picture) VII. Title.
PZ7.7.G55Epl 2009
[Fic]--dc22
                        2008038311

All Spotlight books have reinforced library bindings and are manufactured in the United States of America.

Episode II

ATTACK OF THE CLONES

Volume 2

Senator Amidala has returned to Coruscant to vote against creating an army to assist the Jedi in the fight against the Separatists.

On her arrival, an assassination attempt is made, causing the Supreme Chancellor to assign Jedi Obi-Wan Kenobi, along with his Padawan Anakin Skywalker, to protect her.

In a second attempt on Amidala's life, the Jedi apprehend the bounty hunter, but are unable to discover who is behind the plot. For her safety, Amidala prepares to return to her planet of Naboo with Anakin for protection . . .

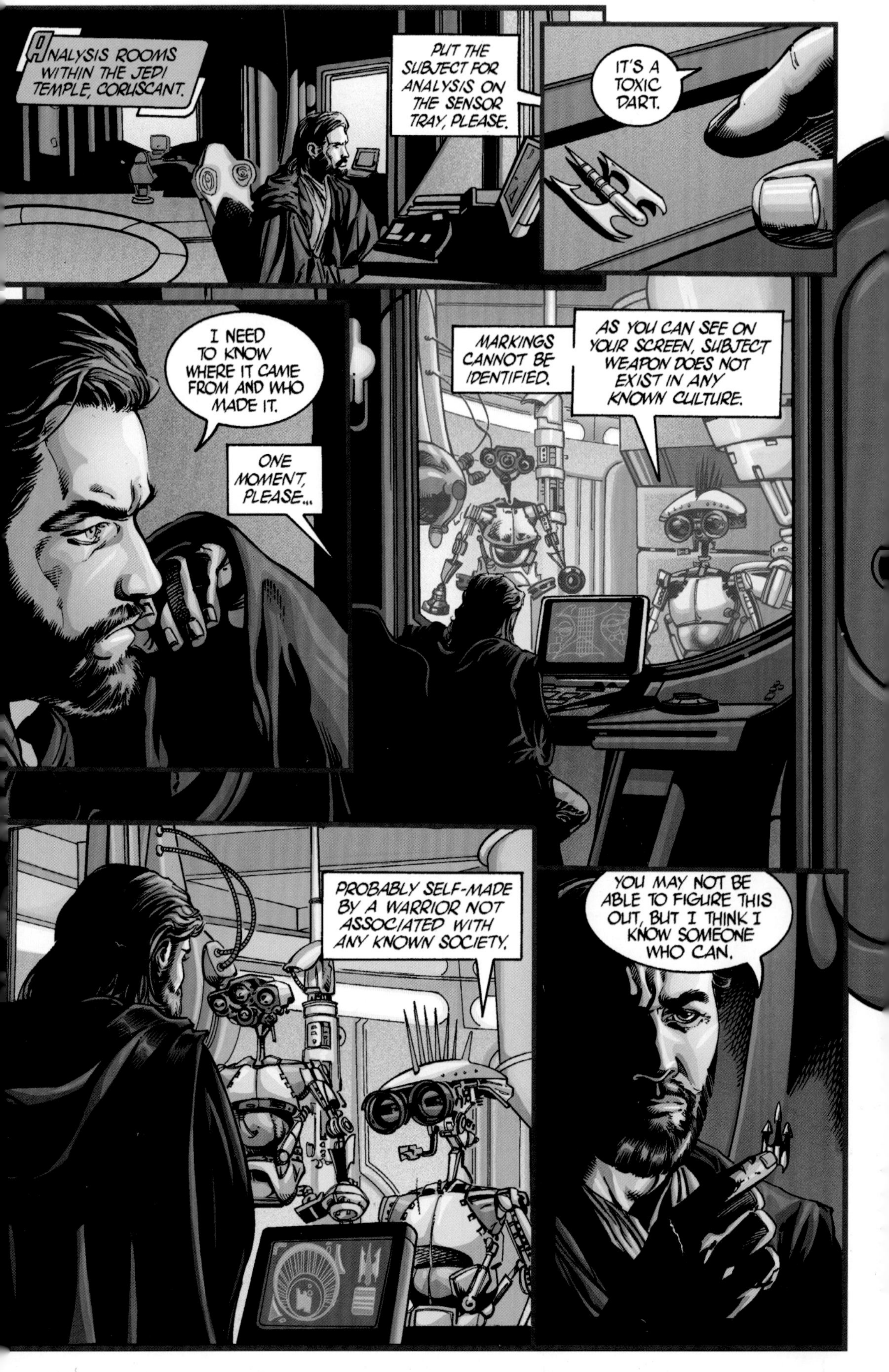
ANALYSIS ROOMS WITHIN THE JEDI TEMPLE, CORUSCANT.
PUT THE SUBJECT FOR ANALYSIS ON THE SENSOR TRAY, PLEASE.
IT'S A TOXIC DART.
I NEED TO KNOW WHERE IT CAME FROM AND WHO MADE IT.
ONE MOMENT, PLEASE...
MARKINGS CANNOT BE IDENTIFIED.
AS YOU CAN SEE ON YOUR SCREEN, SUBJECT WEAPON DOES NOT EXIST IN ANY KNOWN CULTURE.
PROBABLY SELF-MADE BY A WARRIOR NOT ASSOCIATED WITH ANY KNOWN SOCIETY.
YOU MAY NOT BE ABLE TO FIGURE THIS OUT, BUT I THINK I KNOW SOMEONE WHO CAN.

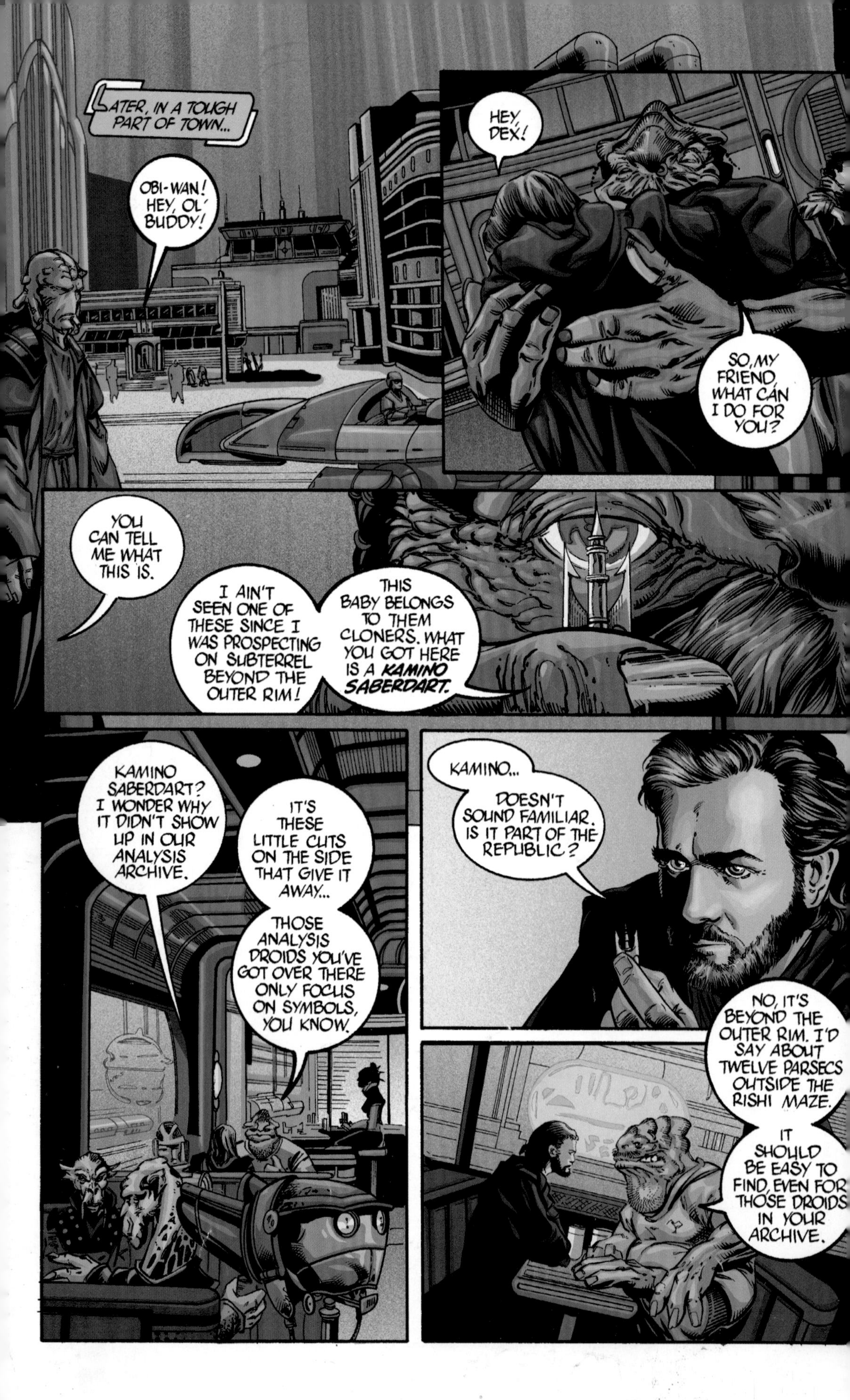
LATER, IN A TOUGH PART OF TOWN...
OBI-WAN! HEY, OL' BUDDY!
HEY, DEX!
SO, MY FRIEND, WHAT CAN I DO FOR YOU?
YOU CAN TELL ME WHAT THIS IS.
I AIN'T SEEN ONE OF THESE SINCE I WAS PROSPECTING ON SUBTERREL BEYOND THE OUTER RIM!
THIS BABY BELONGS TO THEM CLONERS. WHAT YOU GOT HERE IS A KAMINO SABERDART.
KAMINO SABERDART? I WONDER WHY IT DIDN'T SHOW UP IN OUR ANALYSIS ARCHIVE.
IT'S THESE LITTLE CUTS ON THE SIDE THAT GIVE IT AWAY...
THOSE ANALYSIS DROIDS YOU'VE GOT OVER THERE ONLY FOCUS ON SYMBOLS, YOU KNOW.
KAMINO...
DOESN'T SOUND FAMILIAR. IS IT PART OF THE REPUBLIC?
NO, IT'S BEYOND THE OUTER RIM. I'D SAY ABOUT TWELVE PARSECS OUTSIDE THE RISHI MAZE.
IT SHOULD BE EASY TO FIND, EVEN FOR THOSE DROIDS IN YOUR ARCHIVE.

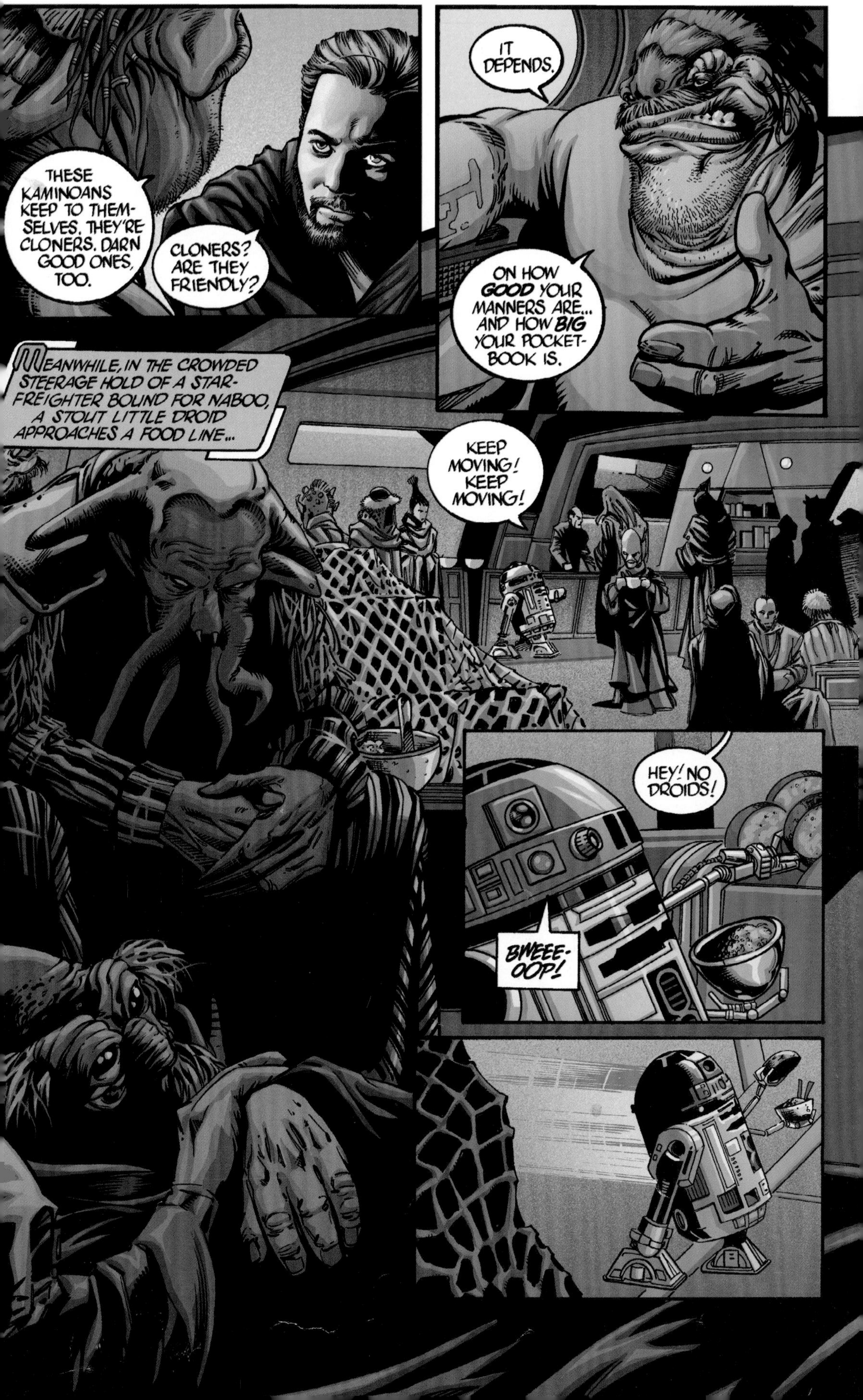
THESE KAMINOANS KEEP TO THEMSELVES, THEY'RE CLONERS. DARN GOOD ONES, TOO.
CLONERS? ARE THEY FRIENDLY?
IT DEPENDS.
ON HOW GOOD YOUR MANNERS ARE... AND HOW BIG YOUR POCKETBOOK IS.
MEANWHILE, IN THE CROWDED STEERAGE HOLD OF A STARFREIGHTER BOUND FOR NABOO, A STOUT LITTLE DROID APPROACHES A FOOD LINE...
KEEP MOVING! KEEP MOVING!
HEY! NO DROIDS!
BWEEE-OOP!

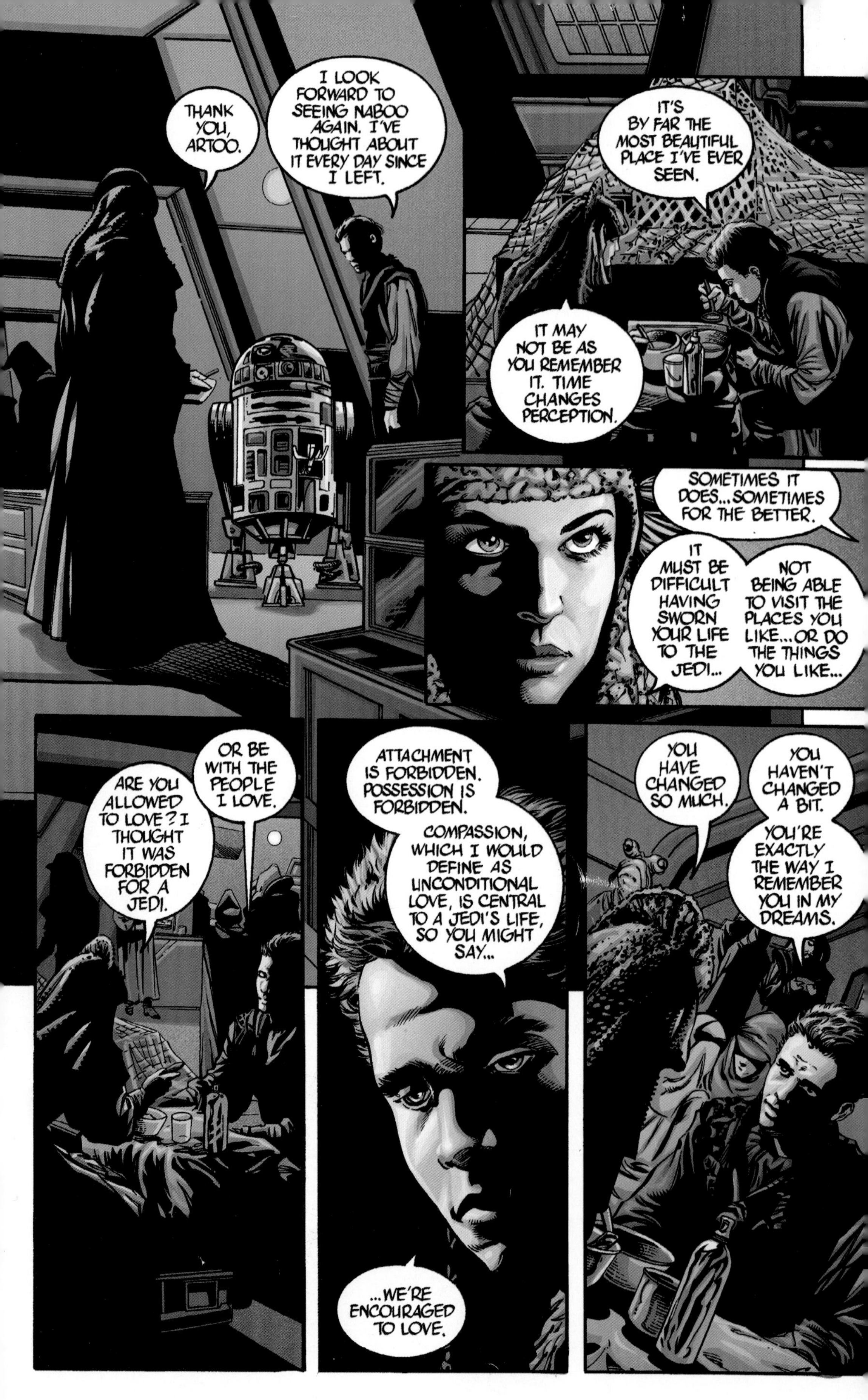
THANK YOU, ARTOO.
I LOOK FORWARD TO SEEING NABOO AGAIN. I'VE THOUGHT ABOUT IT EVERY DAY SINCE I LEFT.
IT'S BY FAR THE MOST BEAUTIFUL PLACE I'VE EVER SEEN.
IT MAY NOT BE AS YOU REMEMBER IT. TIME CHANGES PERCEPTION.
SOMETIMES IT DOES... SOMETIMES FOR THE BETTER.
IT MUST BE DIFFICULT HAVING SWORN YOUR LIFE TO THE JEDI...
NOT BEING ABLE TO VISIT THE PLACES YOU LIKE... OR DO THE THINGS YOU LIKE...
OR BE WITH THE PEOPLE I LOVE.
ARE YOU ALLOWED TO LOVE? I THOUGHT IT WAS FORBIDDEN FOR A JEDI.
ATTACHMENT IS FORBIDDEN. POSSESSION IS FORBIDDEN.
COMPASSION, WHICH I WOULD DEFINE AS UNCONDITIONAL LOVE, IS CENTRAL TO A JEDI'S LIFE, SO YOU MIGHT SAY...
...WE'RE ENCOURAGED TO LOVE.
YOU HAVE CHANGED SO MUCH.
YOU HAVEN'T CHANGED A BIT.
YOU'RE EXACTLY THE WAY I REMEMBER YOU IN MY DREAMS.

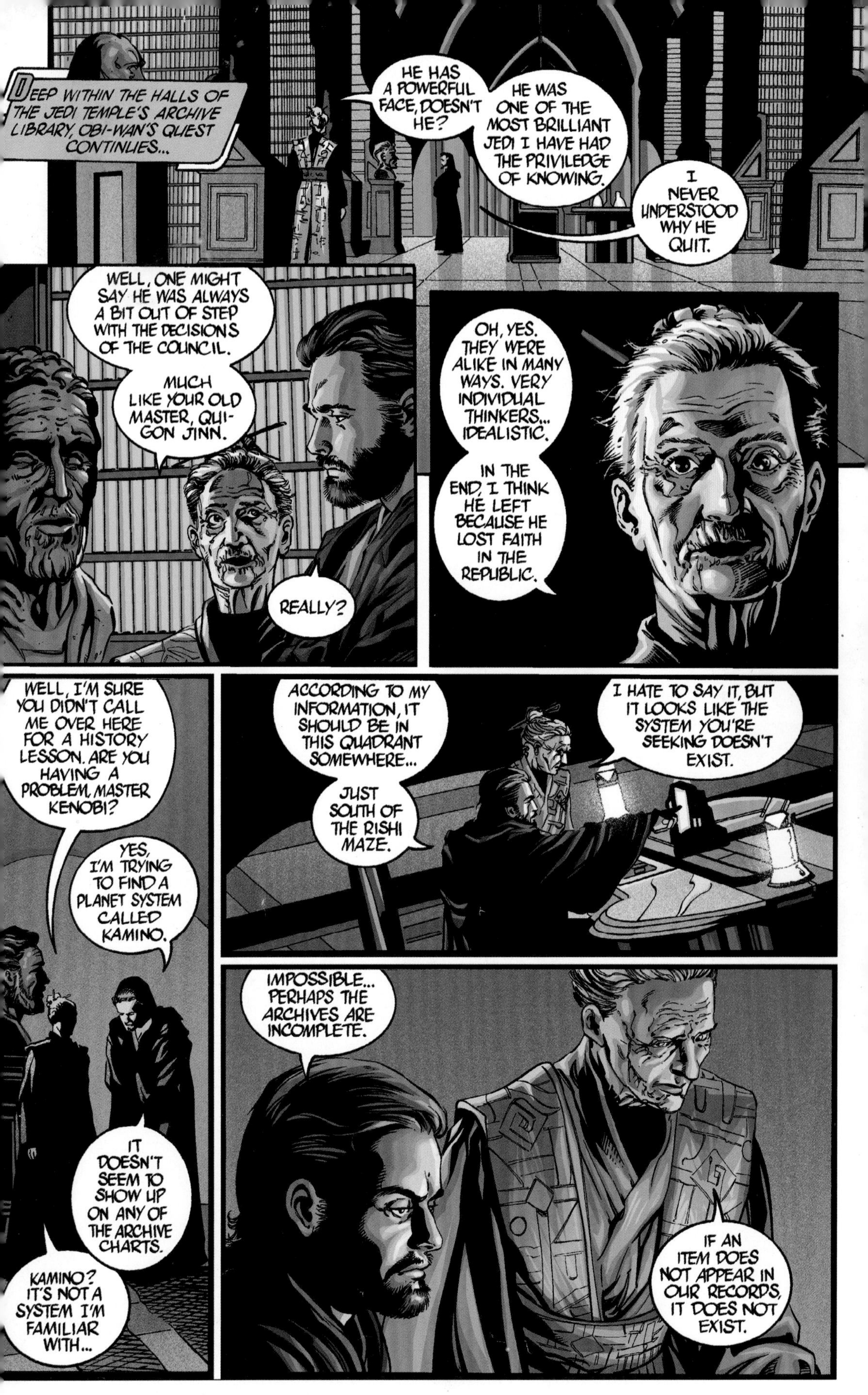
DEEP WITHIN THE HALLS OF THE JEDI TEMPLE'S ARCHIVE LIBRARY, OBI-WAN'S QUEST CONTINUES...
HE HAS A POWERFUL FACE, DOESN'T HE?
HE WAS ONE OF THE MOST BRILLIANT JEDI I HAVE HAD THE PRIVILEDGE OF KNOWING.
I NEVER UNDERSTOOD WHY HE QUIT.
WELL, ONE MIGHT SAY HE WAS ALWAYS A BIT OUT OF STEP WITH THE DECISIONS OF THE COUNCIL.
MUCH LIKE YOUR OLD MASTER, QUI-GON JINN.
REALLY?
OH, YES. THEY WERE ALIKE IN MANY WAYS. VERY INDIVIDUAL THINKERS... IDEALISTIC.
IN THE END, I THINK HE LEFT BECAUSE HE LOST FAITH IN THE REPUBLIC.
WELL, I'M SURE YOU DIDN'T CALL ME OVER HERE FOR A HISTORY LESSON. ARE YOU HAVING A PROBLEM, MASTER KENOBI?
YES, I'M TRYING TO FIND A PLANET SYSTEM CALLED KAMINO.
IT DOESN'T SEEM TO SHOW UP ON ANY OF THE ARCHIVE CHARTS.
KAMINO? IT'S NOT A SYSTEM I'M FAMILIAR WITH...
ACCORDING TO MY INFORMATION, IT SHOULD BE IN THIS QUADRANT SOMEWHERE...
JUST SOUTH OF THE RISHI MAZE.
I HATE TO SAY IT, BUT IT LOOKS LIKE THE SYSTEM YOU'RE SEEKING DOESN'T EXIST.
IMPOSSIBLE... PERHAPS THE ARCHIVES ARE INCOMPLETE.
IF AN ITEM DOES NOT APPEAR IN OUR RECORDS, IT DOES NOT EXIST.

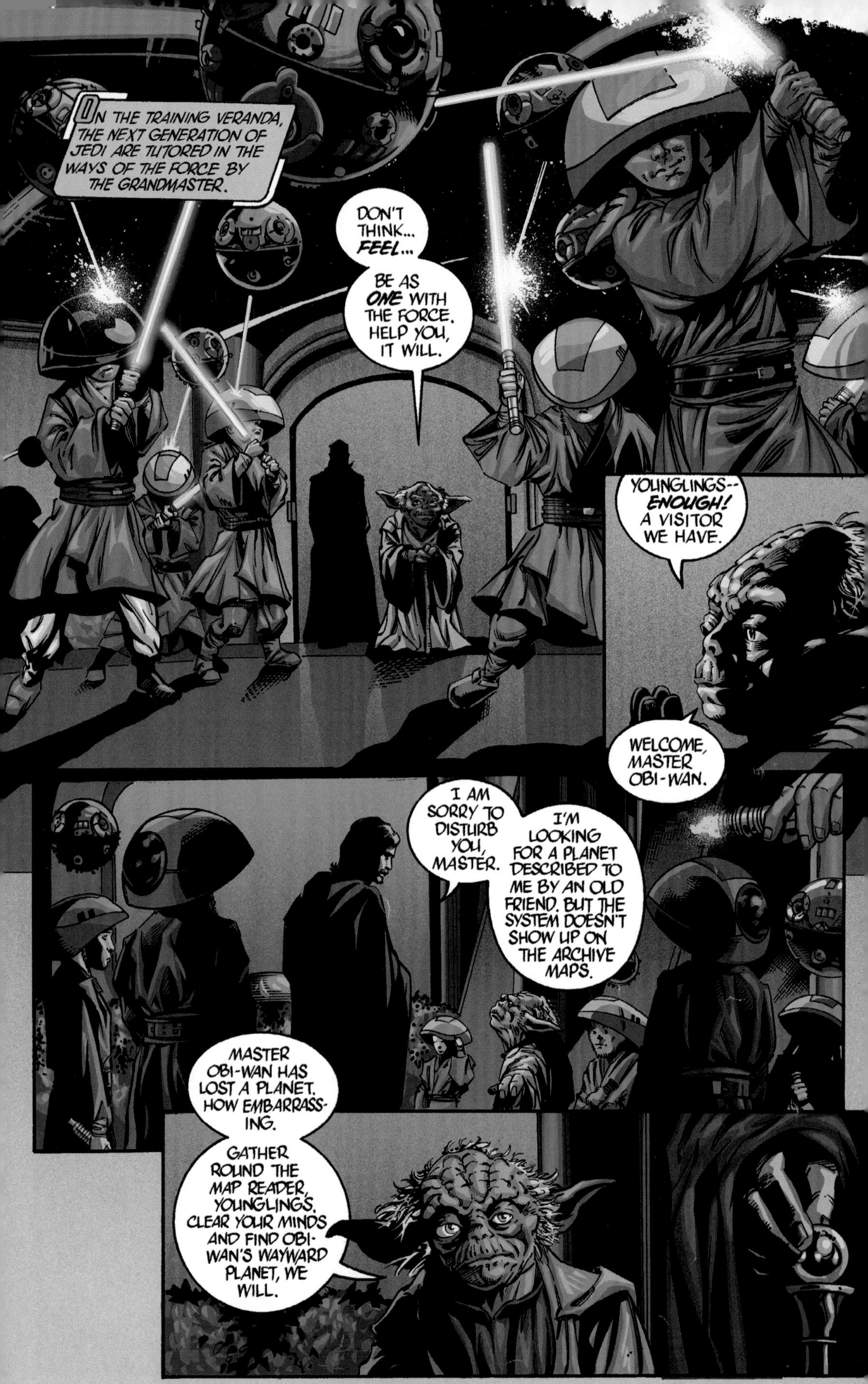
On the training veranda, the next generation of Jedi are tutored in the ways of the Force by the Grandmaster.
DON'T THINK... FEEL...
BE AS ONE WITH THE FORCE. HELP YOU, IT WILL.
YOUNGLINGS-- ENOUGH! A VISITOR WE HAVE.
WELCOME, MASTER OBI-WAN.
I AM SORRY TO DISTURB YOU, MASTER.
I'M LOOKING FOR A PLANET DESCRIBED TO ME BY AN OLD FRIEND. BUT THE SYSTEM DOESN'T SHOW UP ON THE ARCHIVE MAPS.
MASTER OBI-WAN HAS LOST A PLANET. HOW EMBARRASS-ING.
GATHER ROUND THE MAP READER, YOUNGLINGS. CLEAR YOUR MINDS AND FIND OBI-WAN'S WAYWARD PLANET, WE WILL.

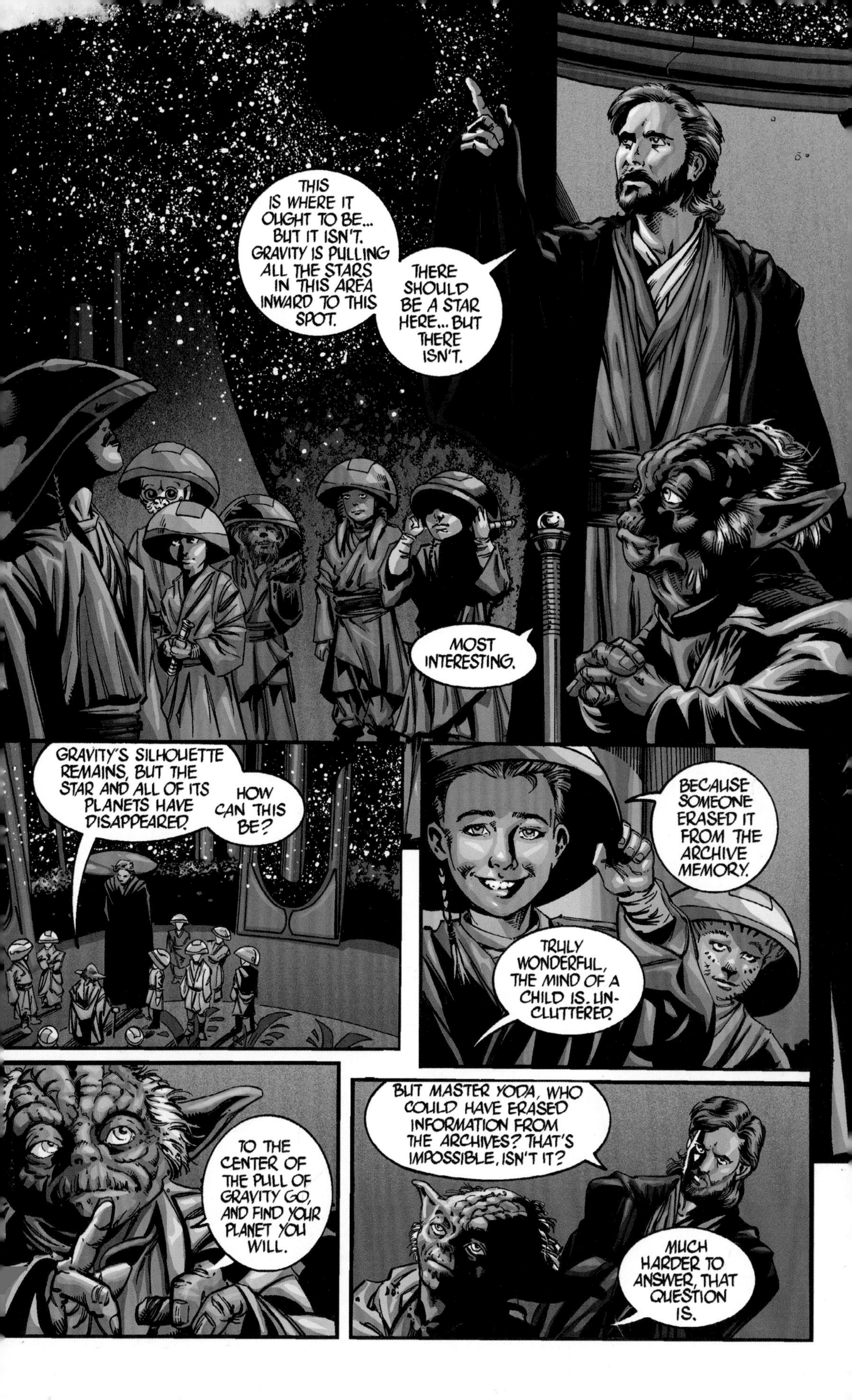
THIS IS WHERE IT OUGHT TO BE... BUT IT ISN'T. GRAVITY IS PULLING ALL THE STARS IN THIS AREA INWARD TO THIS SPOT.
THERE SHOULD BE A STAR HERE... BUT THERE ISN'T.
MOST INTERESTING.
GRAVITY'S SILHOUETTE REMAINS, BUT THE STAR AND ALL OF ITS PLANETS HAVE DISAPPEARED.
HOW CAN THIS BE?
BECAUSE SOMEONE ERASED IT FROM THE ARCHIVE MEMORY.
TRULY WONDERFUL, THE MIND OF A CHILD IS. UN-CLUTTERED.
TO THE CENTER OF THE PULL OF GRAVITY GO, AND FIND YOUR PLANET YOU WILL.
BUT MASTER YODA, WHO COULD HAVE ERASED INFORMATION FROM THE ARCHIVES? THAT'S IMPOSSIBLE, ISN'T IT?
MUCH HARDER TO ANSWER, THAT QUESTION IS.

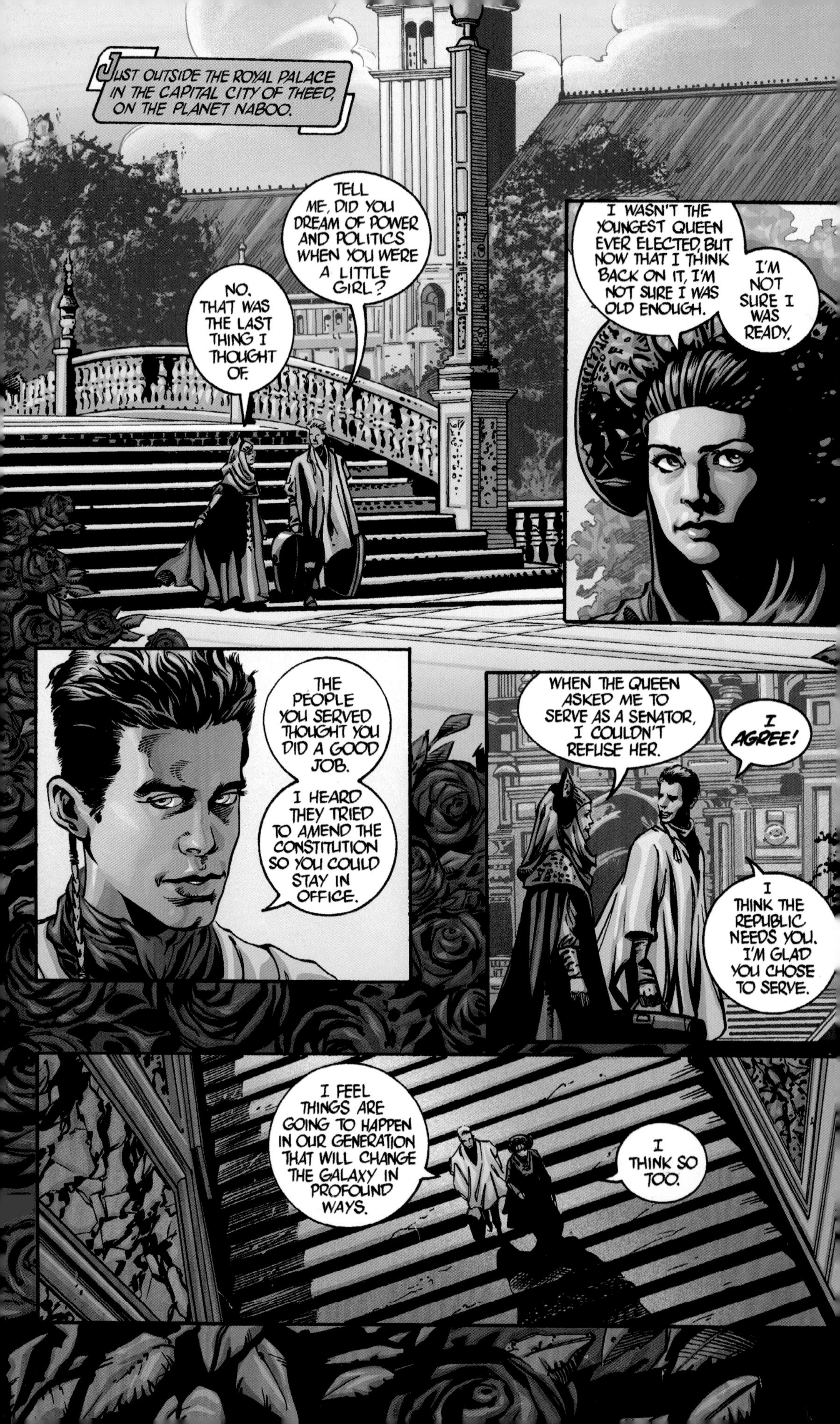
JUST OUTSIDE THE ROYAL PALACE IN THE CAPITAL CITY OF THEED, ON THE PLANET NABOO.
TELL ME, DID YOU DREAM OF POWER AND POLITICS WHEN YOU WERE A LITTLE GIRL?
NO. THAT WAS THE LAST THING I THOUGHT OF.
I WASN'T THE YOUNGEST QUEEN EVER ELECTED, BUT NOW THAT I THINK BACK ON IT, I'M NOT SURE I WAS OLD ENOUGH.
I'M NOT SURE I WAS READY.
THE PEOPLE YOU SERVED THOUGHT YOU DID A GOOD JOB.
I HEARD THEY TRIED TO AMEND THE CONSTITUTION SO YOU COULD STAY IN OFFICE.
WHEN THE QUEEN ASKED ME TO SERVE AS A SENATOR, I COULDN'T REFUSE HER.
I AGREE!
I THINK THE REPUBLIC NEEDS YOU. I'M GLAD YOU CHOSE TO SERVE.
I FEEL THINGS ARE GOING TO HAPPEN IN OUR GENERATION THAT WILL CHANGE THE GALAXY IN PROFOUND WAYS.
I THINK SO TOO.

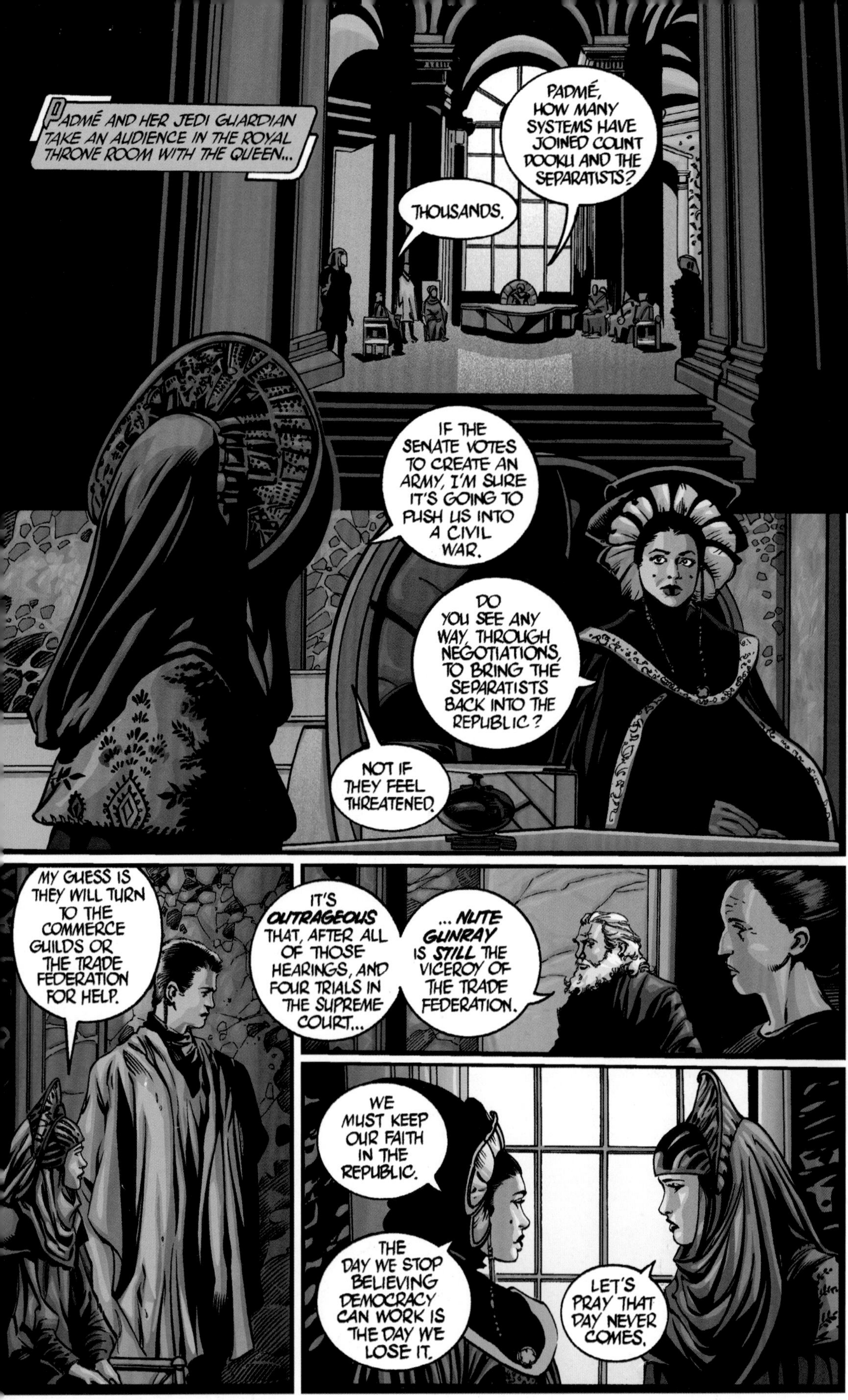
PADMÉ AND HER JEDI GUARDIAN TAKE AN AUDIENCE IN THE ROYAL THRONE ROOM WITH THE QUEEN...
PADMÉ, HOW MANY SYSTEMS HAVE JOINED COUNT DOOKU AND THE SEPARATISTS?
THOUSANDS.
IF THE SENATE VOTES TO CREATE AN ARMY, I'M SURE IT'S GOING TO PUSH US INTO A CIVIL WAR.
DO YOU SEE ANY WAY, THROUGH NEGOTIATIONS, TO BRING THE SEPARATISTS BACK INTO THE REPUBLIC?
NOT IF THEY FEEL THREATENED.
MY GUESS IS THEY WILL TURN TO THE COMMERCE GUILDS OR THE TRADE FEDERATION FOR HELP.
IT'S OUTRAGEOUS THAT, AFTER ALL OF THOSE HEARINGS, AND FOUR TRIALS IN THE SUPREME COURT...
...NUTE GUNRAY IS STILL THE VICEROY OF THE TRADE FEDERATION.
WE MUST KEEP OUR FAITH IN THE REPUBLIC.
THE DAY WE STOP BELIEVING DEMOCRACY CAN WORK IS THE DAY WE LOSE IT.
LET'S PRAY THAT DAY NEVER COMES.

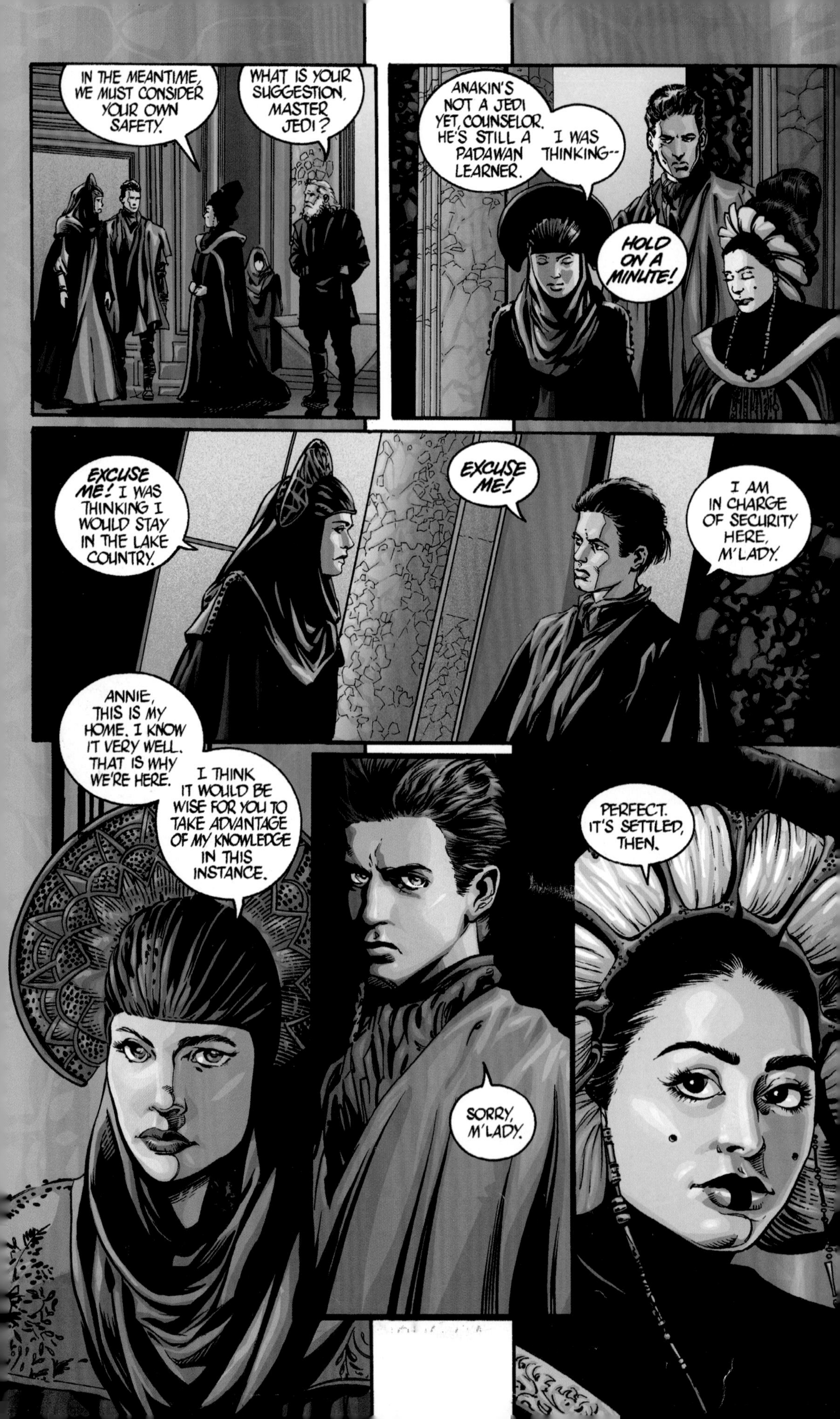
IN THE MEANTIME, WE MUST CONSIDER YOUR OWN SAFETY.
WHAT IS YOUR SUGGESTION, MASTER JEDI?
ANAKIN'S NOT A JEDI YET, COUNSELOR. HE'S STILL A PADAWAN LEARNER.
I WAS THINKING--
HOLD ON A MINUTE!
EXCUSE ME! I WAS THINKING I WOULD STAY IN THE LAKE COUNTRY.
EXCUSE ME!
I AM IN CHARGE OF SECURITY HERE, M'LADY.
ANNIE, THIS IS MY HOME. I KNOW IT VERY WELL. THAT IS WHY WE'RE HERE.
I THINK IT WOULD BE WISE FOR YOU TO TAKE ADVANTAGE OF MY KNOWLEDGE IN THIS INSTANCE.
SORRY, M'LADY.
PERFECT. IT'S SETTLED, THEN.

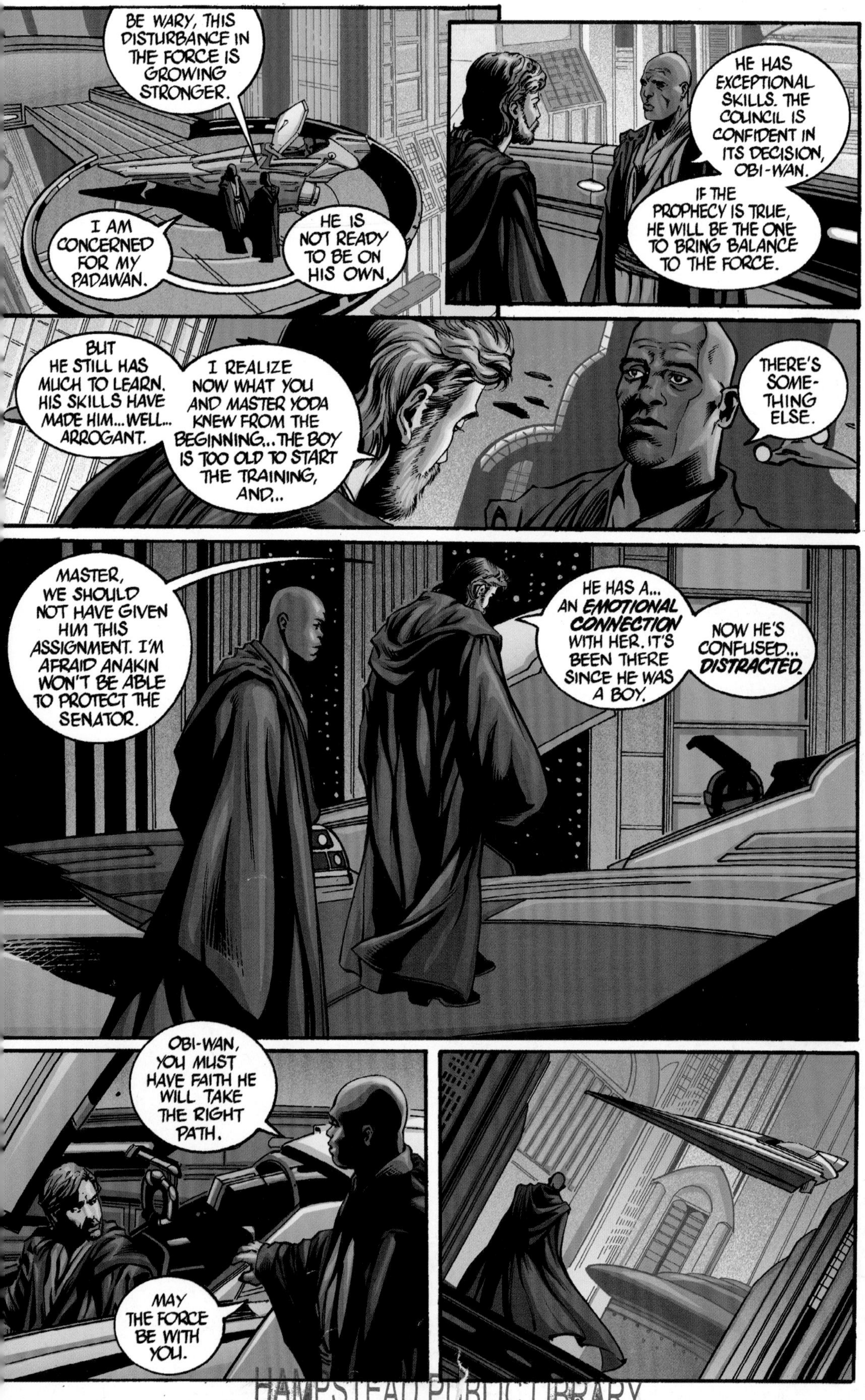
BE WARY, THIS DISTURBANCE IN THE FORCE IS GROWING STRONGER.
I AM CONCERNED FOR MY PADAWAN.
HE IS NOT READY TO BE ON HIS OWN.
HE HAS EXCEPTIONAL SKILLS. THE COUNCIL IS CONFIDENT IN ITS DECISION, OBI-WAN.
IF THE PROPHECY IS TRUE, HE WILL BE THE ONE TO BRING BALANCE TO THE FORCE.
BUT HE STILL HAS MUCH TO LEARN. HIS SKILLS HAVE MADE HIM...WELL... ARROGANT.
I REALIZE NOW WHAT YOU AND MASTER YODA KNEW FROM THE BEGINNING...THE BOY IS TOO OLD TO START THE TRAINING, AND...
THERE'S SOME-THING ELSE.
MASTER, WE SHOULD NOT HAVE GIVEN HIM THIS ASSIGNMENT. I'M AFRAID ANAKIN WON'T BE ABLE TO PROTECT THE SENATOR.
HE HAS A... AN *EMOTIONAL CONNECTION* WITH HER. IT'S BEEN THERE SINCE HE WAS A BOY.
NOW HE'S CONFUSED... *DISTRACTED.*
OBI-WAN, YOU MUST HAVE FAITH HE WILL TAKE THE RIGHT PATH.
MAY THE FORCE BE WITH YOU.

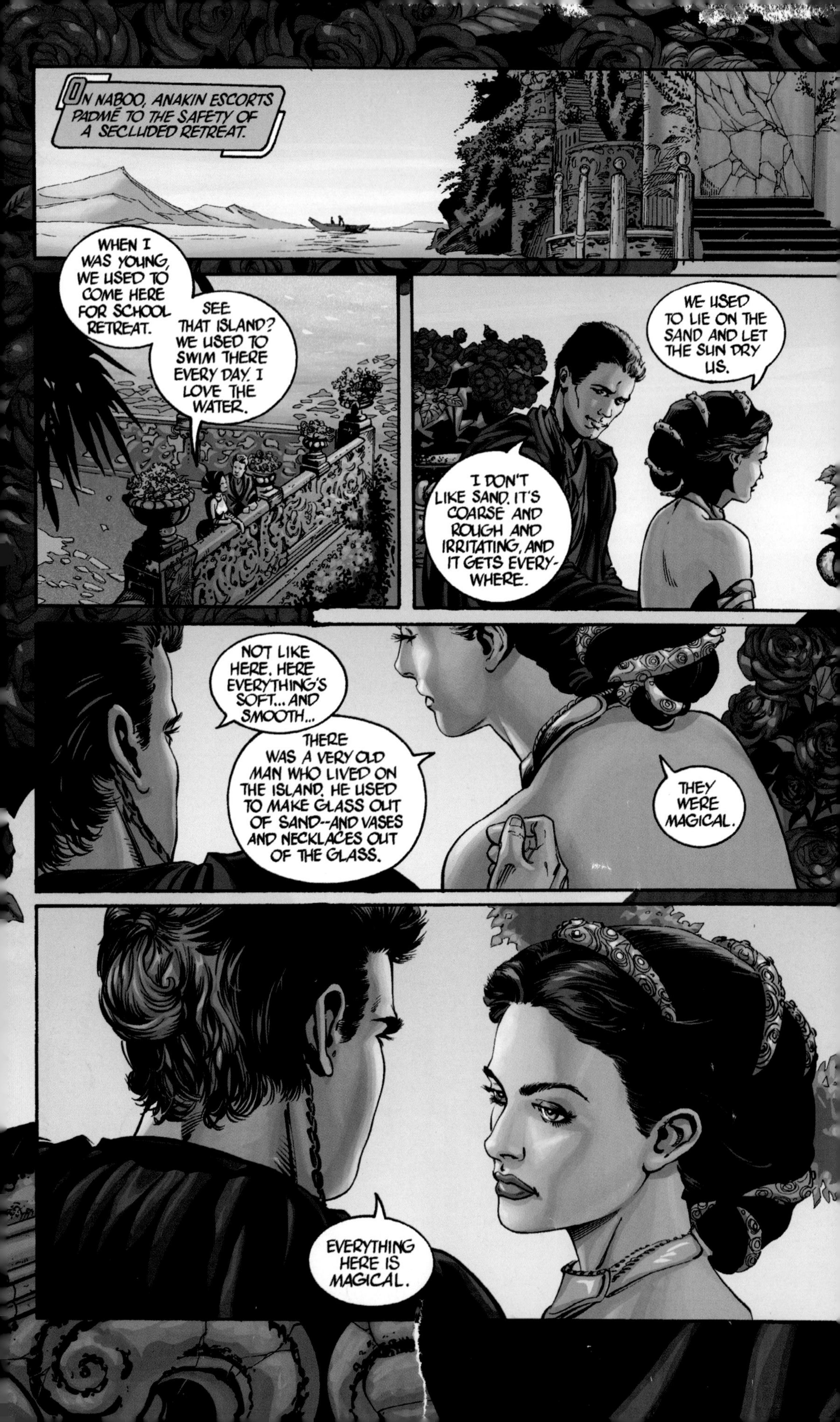
ON NABOO, ANAKIN ESCORTS PADMÉ TO THE SAFETY OF A SECLUDED RETREAT.
WHEN I WAS YOUNG, WE USED TO COME HERE FOR SCHOOL RETREAT.
SEE THAT ISLAND? WE USED TO SWIM THERE EVERY DAY. I LOVE THE WATER.
WE USED TO LIE ON THE SAND AND LET THE SUN DRY US.
I DON'T LIKE SAND. IT'S COARSE AND ROUGH AND IRRITATING, AND IT GETS EVERY-WHERE.
NOT LIKE HERE. HERE EVERYTHING'S SOFT... AND SMOOTH...
THERE WAS A VERY OLD MAN WHO LIVED ON THE ISLAND. HE USED TO MAKE GLASS OUT OF SAND--AND VASES AND NECKLACES OUT OF THE GLASS.
THEY WERE MAGICAL.
EVERYTHING HERE IS MAGICAL.

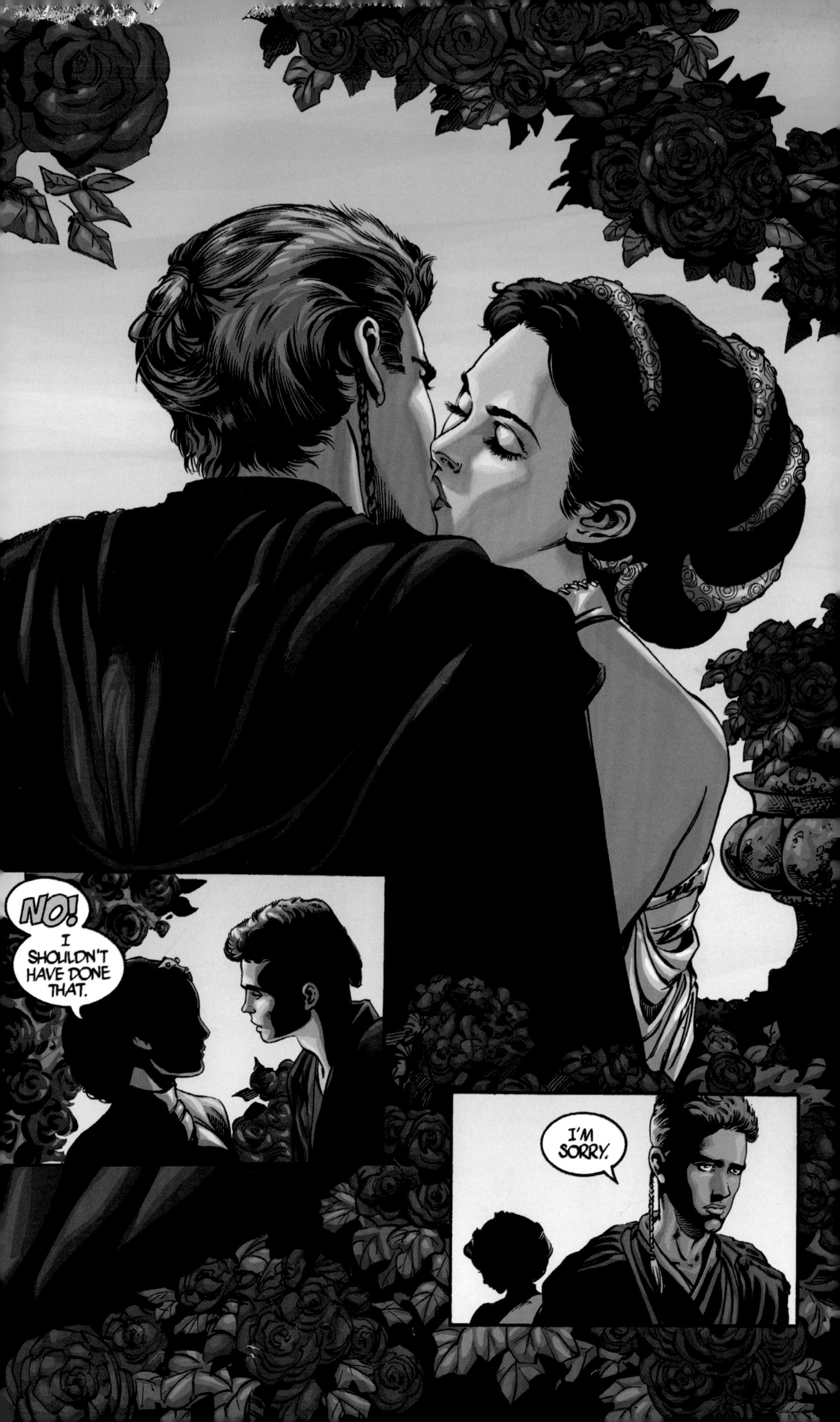
NO! I SHOULDN'T HAVE DONE THAT.
I'M SORRY.

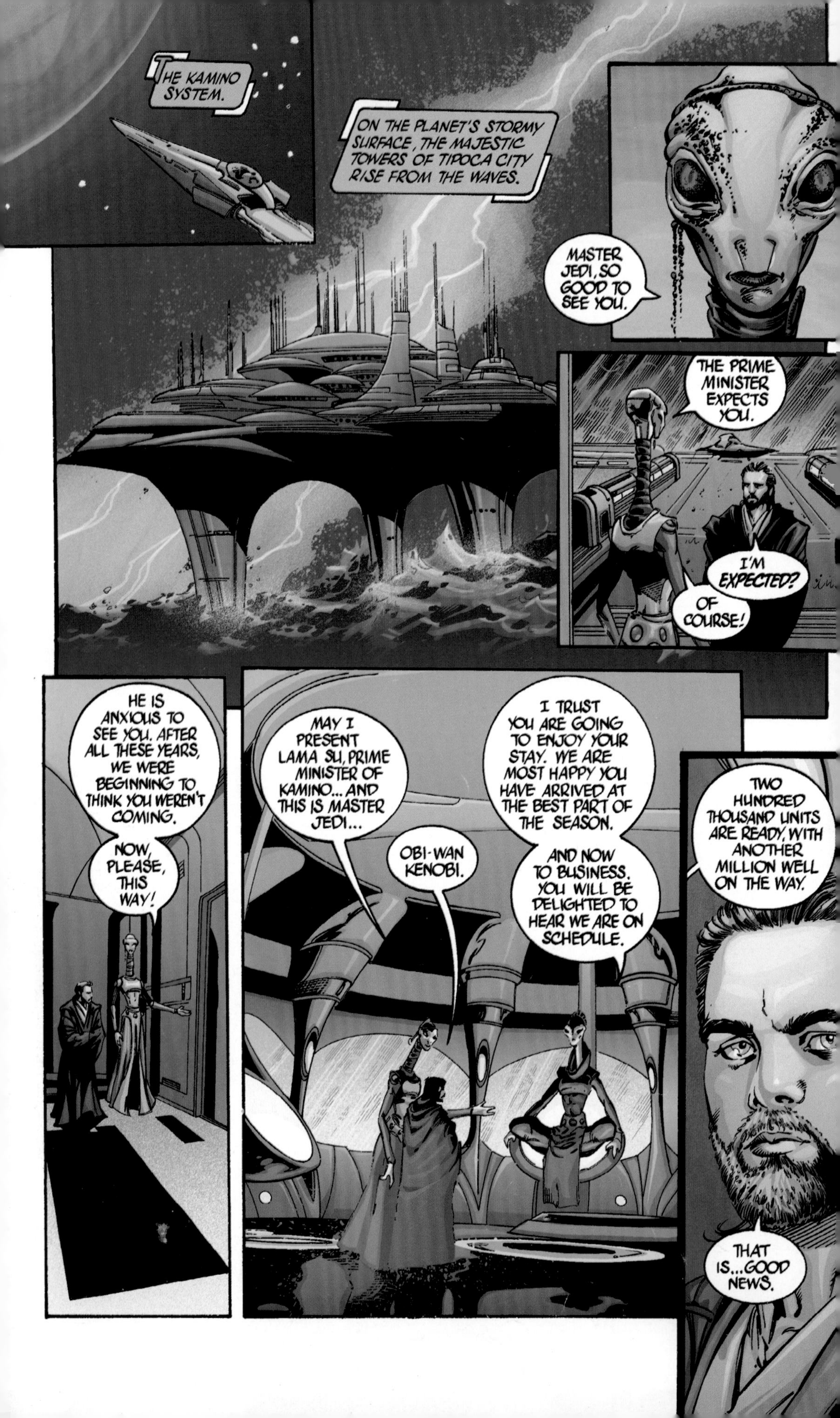
THE KAMINO SYSTEM.
ON THE PLANET'S STORMY SURFACE, THE MAJESTIC TOWERS OF TIPOCA CITY RISE FROM THE WAVES.
MASTER JEDI, SO GOOD TO SEE YOU.
THE PRIME MINISTER EXPECTS YOU.
I'M EXPECTED?
OF COURSE!
HE IS ANXIOUS TO SEE YOU. AFTER ALL THESE YEARS, WE WERE BEGINNING TO THINK YOU WEREN'T COMING.
NOW, PLEASE, THIS WAY!
MAY I PRESENT LAMA SU, PRIME MINISTER OF KAMINO... AND THIS IS MASTER JEDI...
OBI-WAN KENOBI.
I TRUST YOU ARE GOING TO ENJOY YOUR STAY. WE ARE MOST HAPPY YOU HAVE ARRIVED AT THE BEST PART OF THE SEASON.
AND NOW TO BUSINESS. YOU WILL BE DELIGHTED TO HEAR WE ARE ON SCHEDULE.
TWO HUNDRED THOUSAND UNITS ARE READY, WITH ANOTHER MILLION WELL ON THE WAY.
THAT IS...GOOD NEWS.

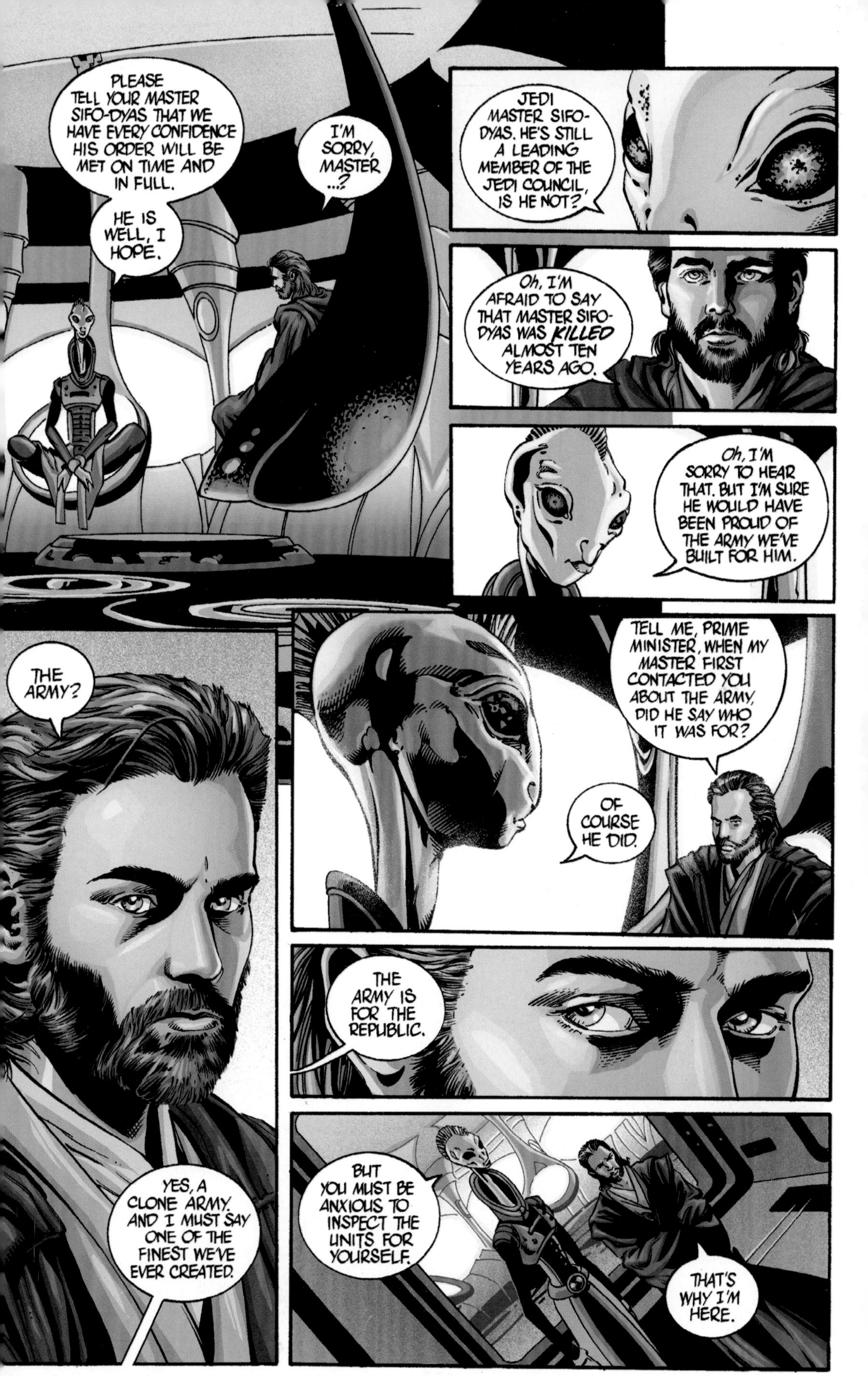
PLEASE TELL YOUR MASTER SIFO-DYAS THAT WE HAVE EVERY CONFIDENCE HIS ORDER WILL BE MET ON TIME AND IN FULL.
HE IS WELL, I HOPE.
I'M SORRY, MASTER ...?
JEDI MASTER SIFO-DYAS. HE'S STILL A LEADING MEMBER OF THE JEDI COUNCIL, IS HE NOT?
Oh, I'M AFRAID TO SAY THAT MASTER SIFO-DYAS WAS KILLED ALMOST TEN YEARS AGO.
Oh, I'M SORRY TO HEAR THAT. BUT I'M SURE HE WOULD HAVE BEEN PROUD OF THE ARMY WE'VE BUILT FOR HIM.
THE ARMY?
YES, A CLONE ARMY. AND I MUST SAY ONE OF THE FINEST WE'VE EVER CREATED.
TELL ME, PRIME MINISTER, WHEN MY MASTER FIRST CONTACTED YOU ABOUT THE ARMY, DID HE SAY WHO IT WAS FOR?
OF COURSE HE DID.
THE ARMY IS FOR THE REPUBLIC.
BUT YOU MUST BE ANXIOUS TO INSPECT THE UNITS FOR YOURSELF.
THAT'S WHY I'M HERE.

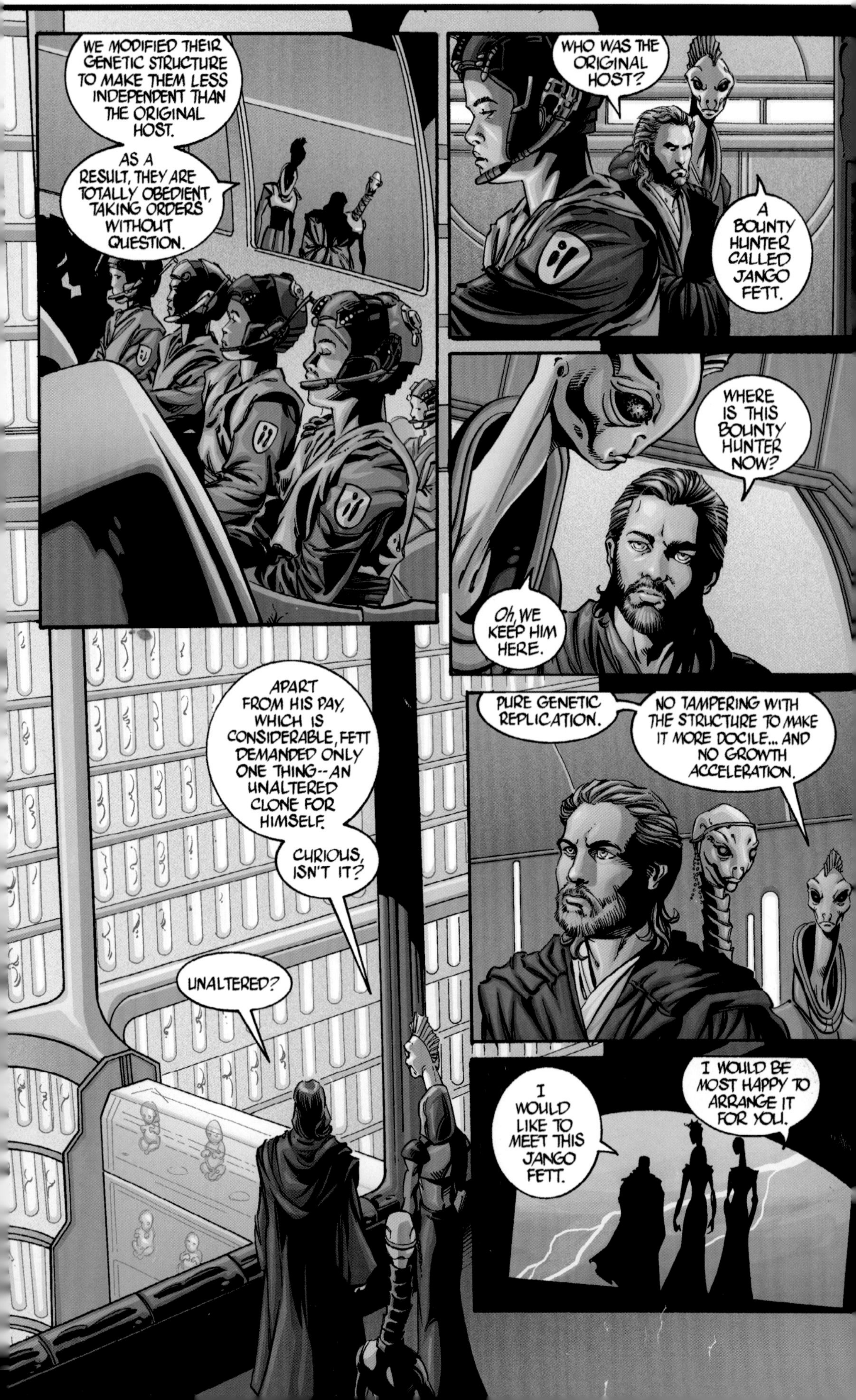
WE MODIFIED THEIR GENETIC STRUCTURE TO MAKE THEM LESS INDEPENDENT THAN THE ORIGINAL HOST.
AS A RESULT, THEY ARE TOTALLY OBEDIENT, TAKING ORDERS WITHOUT QUESTION.
WHO WAS THE ORIGINAL HOST?
A BOUNTY HUNTER CALLED JANGO FETT.
WHERE IS THIS BOUNTY HUNTER NOW?
Oh, WE KEEP HIM HERE.
APART FROM HIS PAY, WHICH IS CONSIDERABLE, FETT DEMANDED ONLY ONE THING--AN UNALTERED CLONE FOR HIMSELF.
CURIOUS, ISN'T IT?
UNALTERED?
PURE GENETIC REPLICATION.
NO TAMPERING WITH THE STRUCTURE TO MAKE IT MORE DOCILE... AND NO GROWTH ACCELERATION.
I WOULD LIKE TO MEET THIS JANGO FETT.
I WOULD BE MOST HAPPY TO ARRANGE IT FOR YOU.

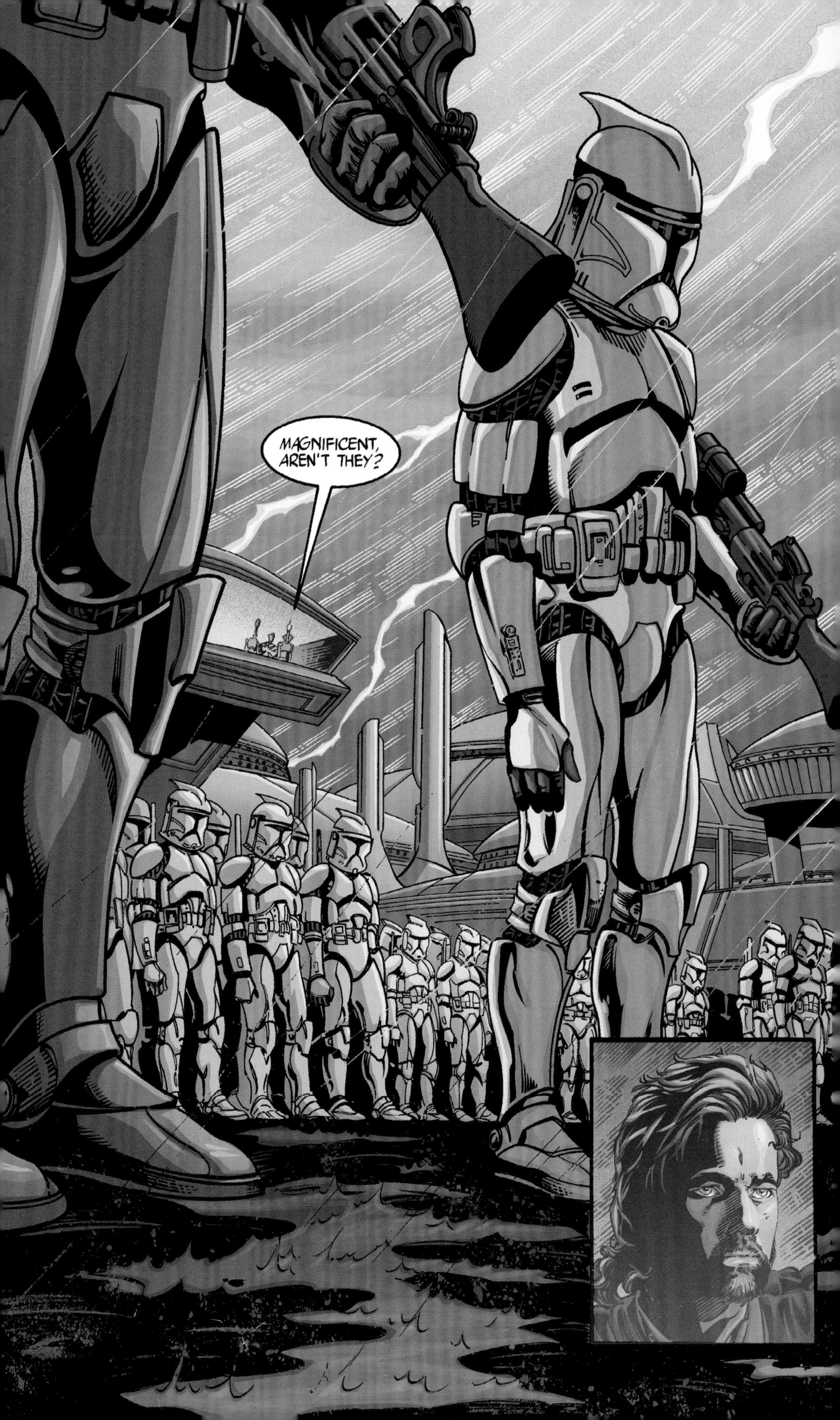
MAGNIFICENT, AREN'T THEY?

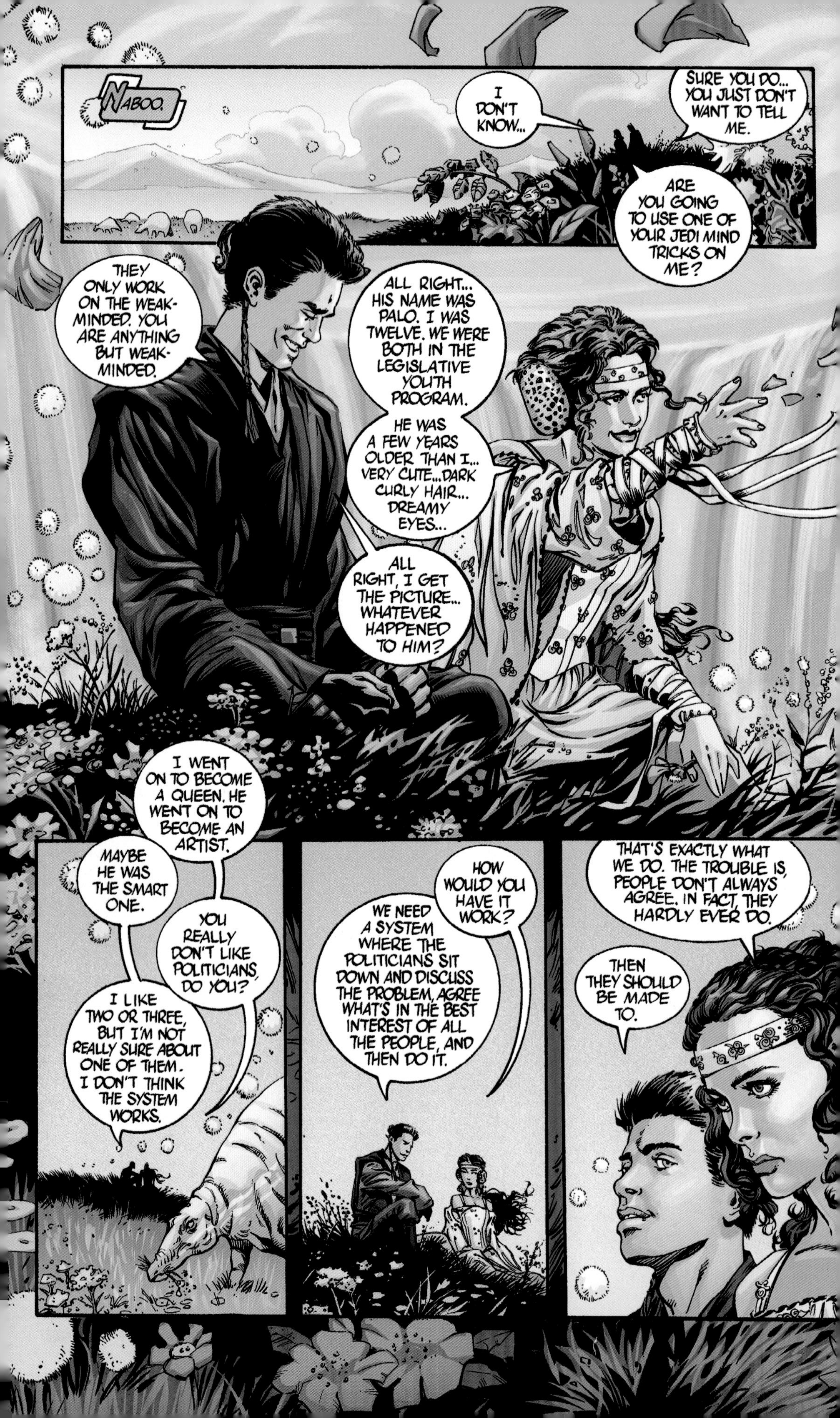
NABOO.
I DON'T KNOW...
SURE YOU DO... YOU JUST DON'T WANT TO TELL ME.
ARE YOU GOING TO USE ONE OF YOUR JEDI MIND TRICKS ON ME?
THEY ONLY WORK ON THE WEAK-MINDED. YOU ARE ANYTHING BUT WEAK-MINDED.
ALL RIGHT... HIS NAME WAS PALO. I WAS TWELVE. WE WERE BOTH IN THE LEGISLATIVE YOUTH PROGRAM.
HE WAS A FEW YEARS OLDER THAN I... VERY CUTE...DARK CURLY HAIR... DREAMY EYES...
ALL RIGHT, I GET THE PICTURE... WHATEVER HAPPENED TO HIM?
I WENT ON TO BECOME A QUEEN. HE WENT ON TO BECOME AN ARTIST.
MAYBE HE WAS THE SMART ONE.
YOU REALLY DON'T LIKE POLITICIANS, DO YOU?
I LIKE TWO OR THREE, BUT I'M NOT REALLY SURE ABOUT ONE OF THEM. I DON'T THINK THE SYSTEM WORKS.
HOW WOULD YOU HAVE IT WORK?
WE NEED A SYSTEM WHERE THE POLITICIANS SIT DOWN AND DISCUSS THE PROBLEM, AGREE WHAT'S IN THE BEST INTEREST OF ALL THE PEOPLE, AND THEN DO IT.
THAT'S EXACTLY WHAT WE DO. THE TROUBLE IS, PEOPLE DON'T ALWAYS AGREE. IN FACT, THEY HARDLY EVER DO.
THEN THEY SHOULD BE MADE TO.

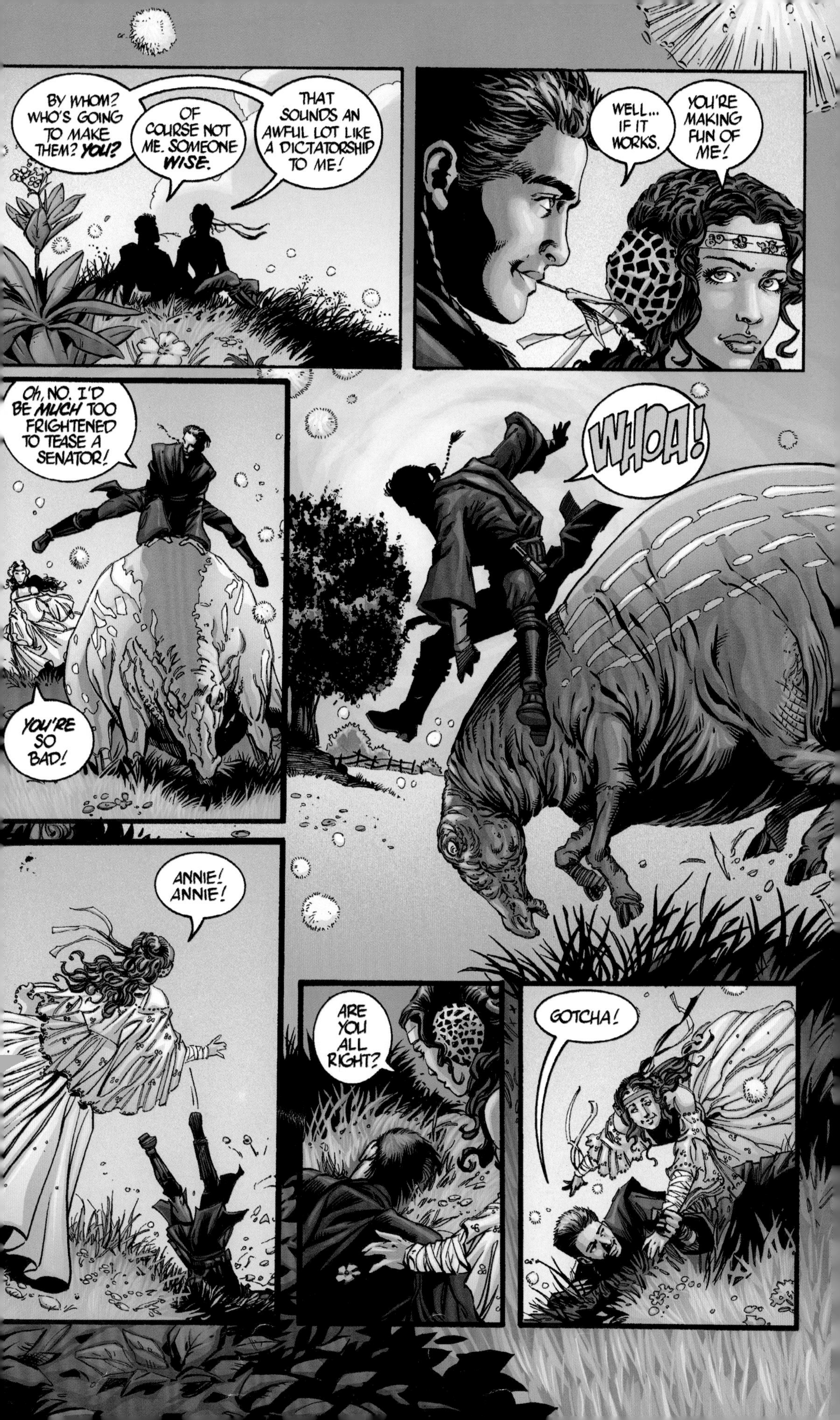
BY WHOM? WHO'S GOING TO MAKE THEM? YOU?
OF COURSE NOT ME. SOMEONE WISE.
THAT SOUNDS AN AWFUL LOT LIKE A DICTATORSHIP TO ME!
WELL... IF IT WORKS.
YOU'RE MAKING FUN OF ME!
OH, NO. I'D BE MUCH TOO FRIGHTENED TO TEASE A SENATOR!
YOU'RE SO BAD!
WHOA!
ANNIE! ANNIE!
ARE YOU ALL RIGHT?
GOTCHA!

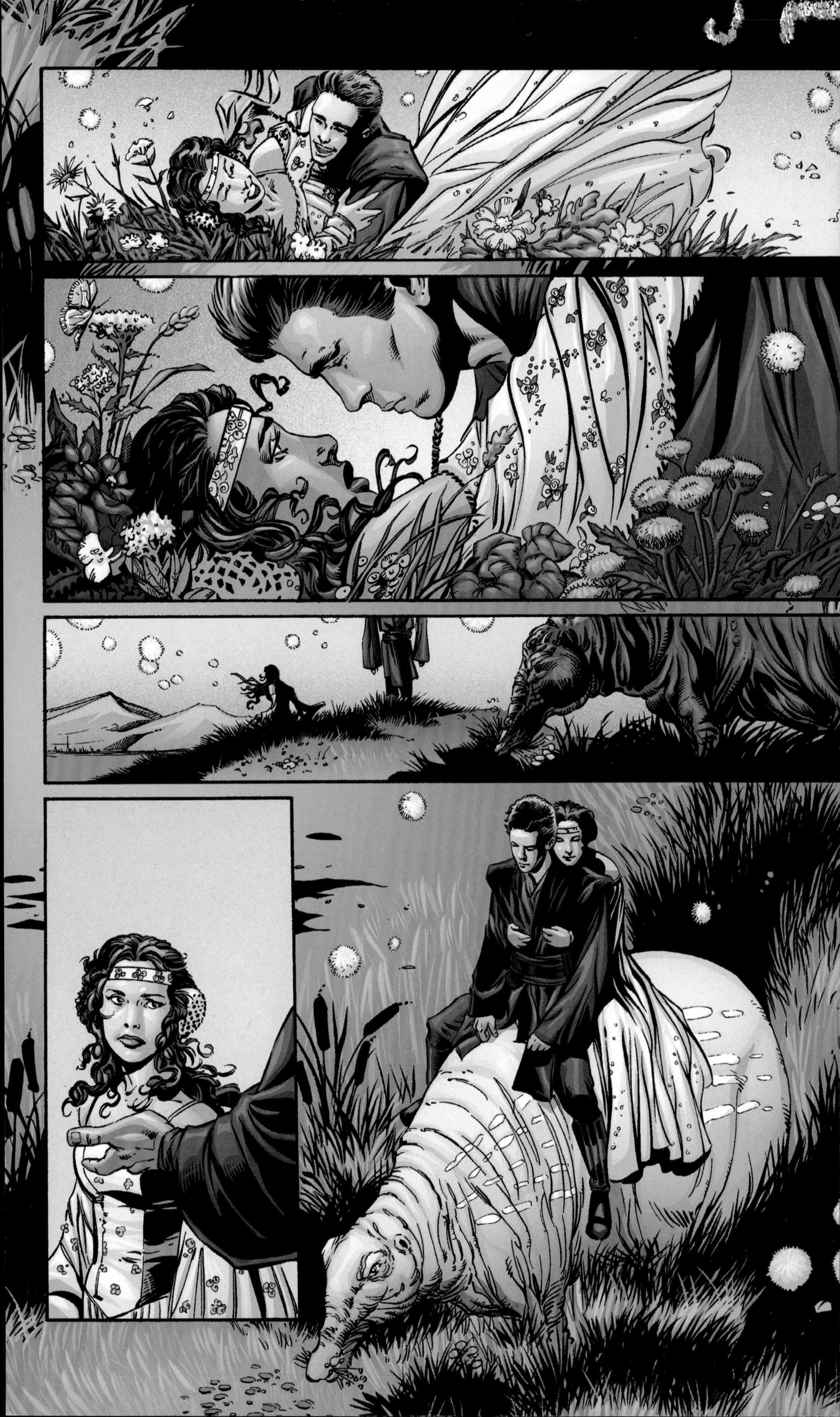

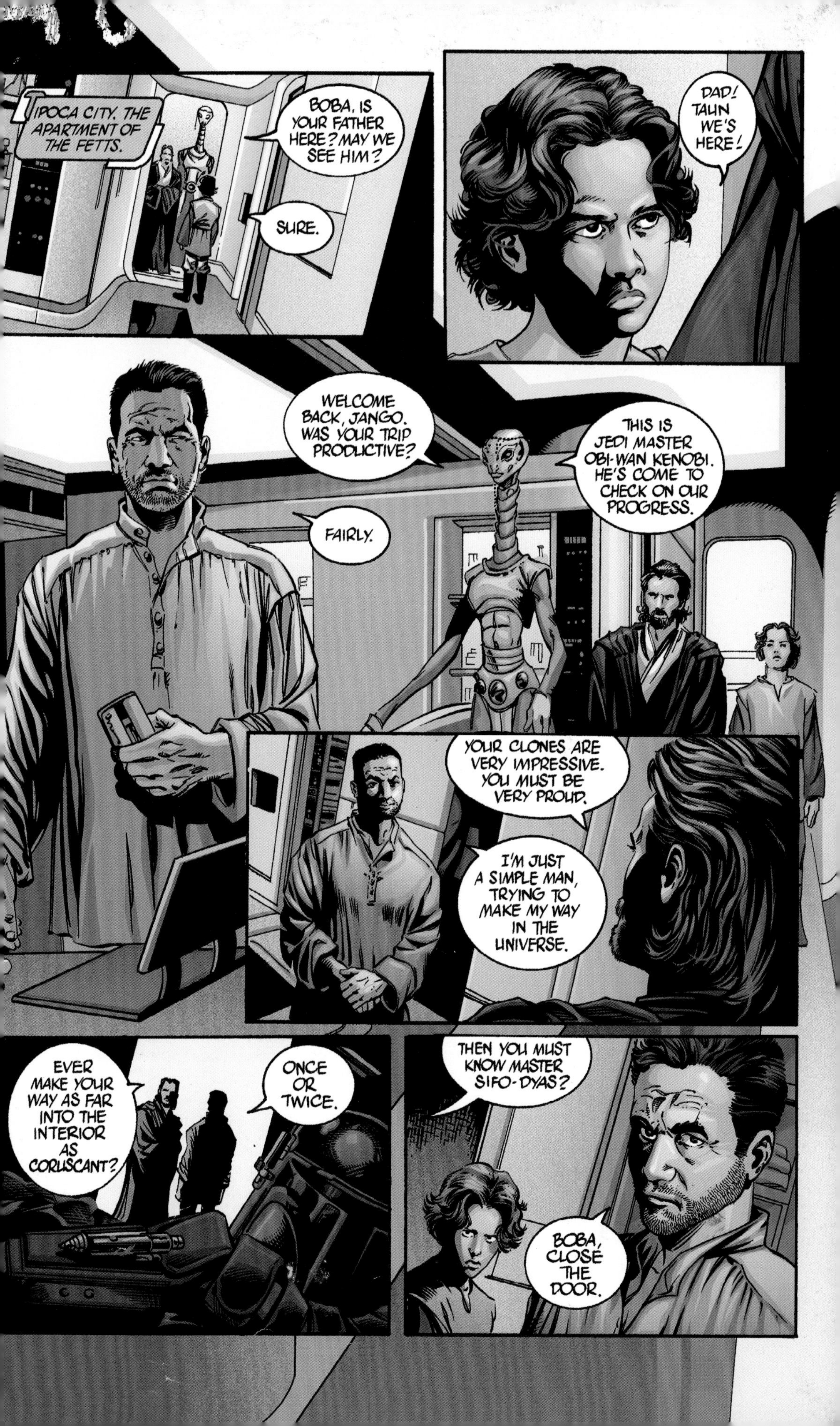

TIPOCA CITY. THE APARTMENT OF THE FETTS.
BOBA, IS YOUR FATHER HERE? MAY WE SEE HIM?
SURE.
DAD! TAUN WE'S HERE!
WELCOME BACK, JANGO. WAS YOUR TRIP PRODUCTIVE?
FAIRLY.
THIS IS JEDI MASTER OBI-WAN KENOBI. HE'S COME TO CHECK ON OUR PROGRESS.
YOUR CLONES ARE VERY IMPRESSIVE. YOU MUST BE VERY PROUD.
I'M JUST A SIMPLE MAN, TRYING TO MAKE MY WAY IN THE UNIVERSE.
EVER MAKE YOUR WAY AS FAR INTO THE INTERIOR AS CORUSCANT?
ONCE OR TWICE.
THEN YOU MUST KNOW MASTER SIFO-DYAS?
BOBA, CLOSE THE DOOR.

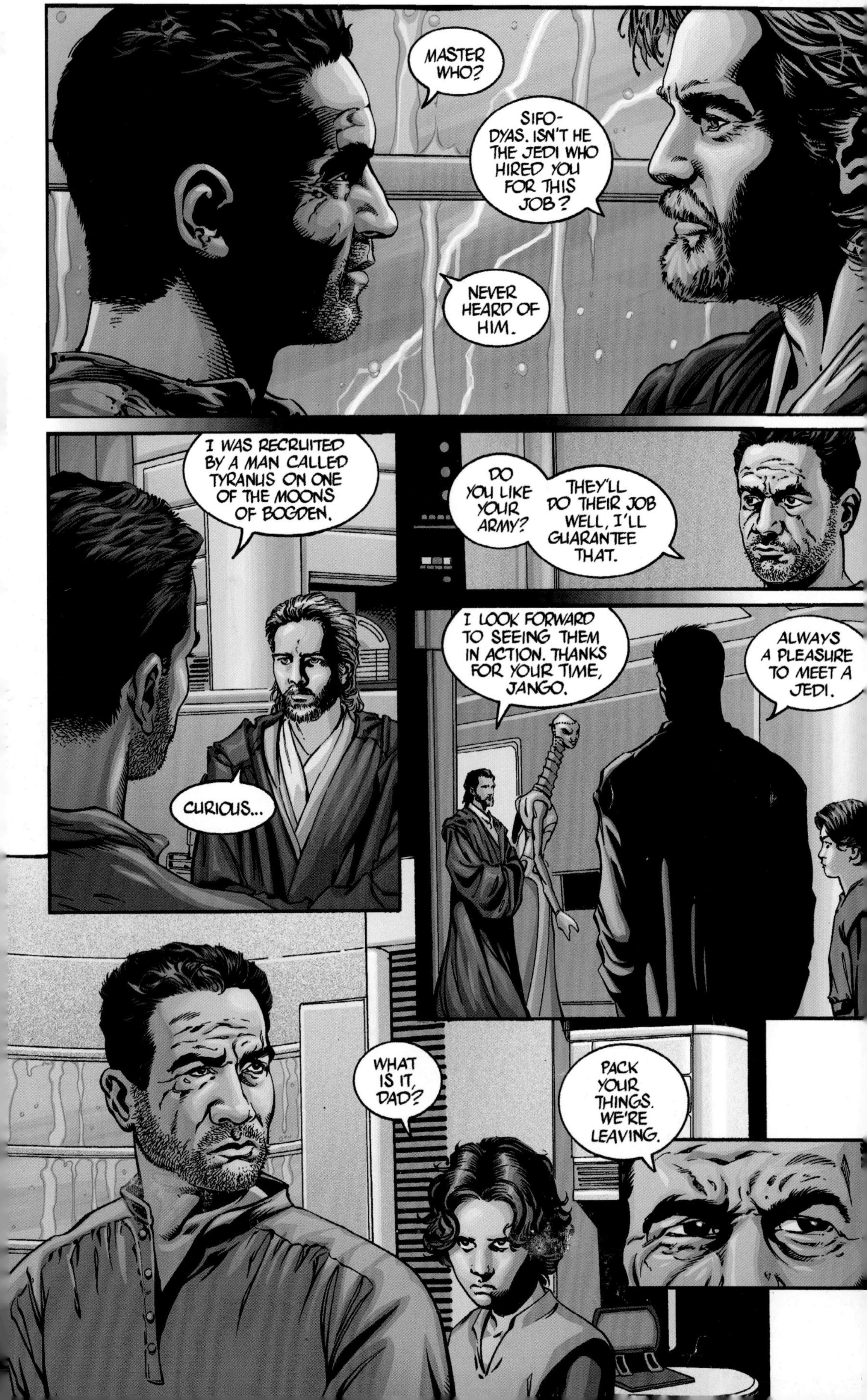
MASTER WHO?
SIFO-DYAS. ISN'T HE THE JEDI WHO HIRED YOU FOR THIS JOB?
NEVER HEARD OF HIM.
I WAS RECRUITED BY A MAN CALLED TYRANUS ON ONE OF THE MOONS OF BOGDEN.
CURIOUS...
DO YOU LIKE YOUR ARMY?
THEY'LL DO THEIR JOB WELL, I'LL GUARANTEE THAT.
I LOOK FORWARD TO SEEING THEM IN ACTION. THANKS FOR YOUR TIME, JANGO.
ALWAYS A PLEASURE TO MEET A JEDI.
WHAT IS IT, DAD?
PACK YOUR THINGS. WE'RE LEAVING.

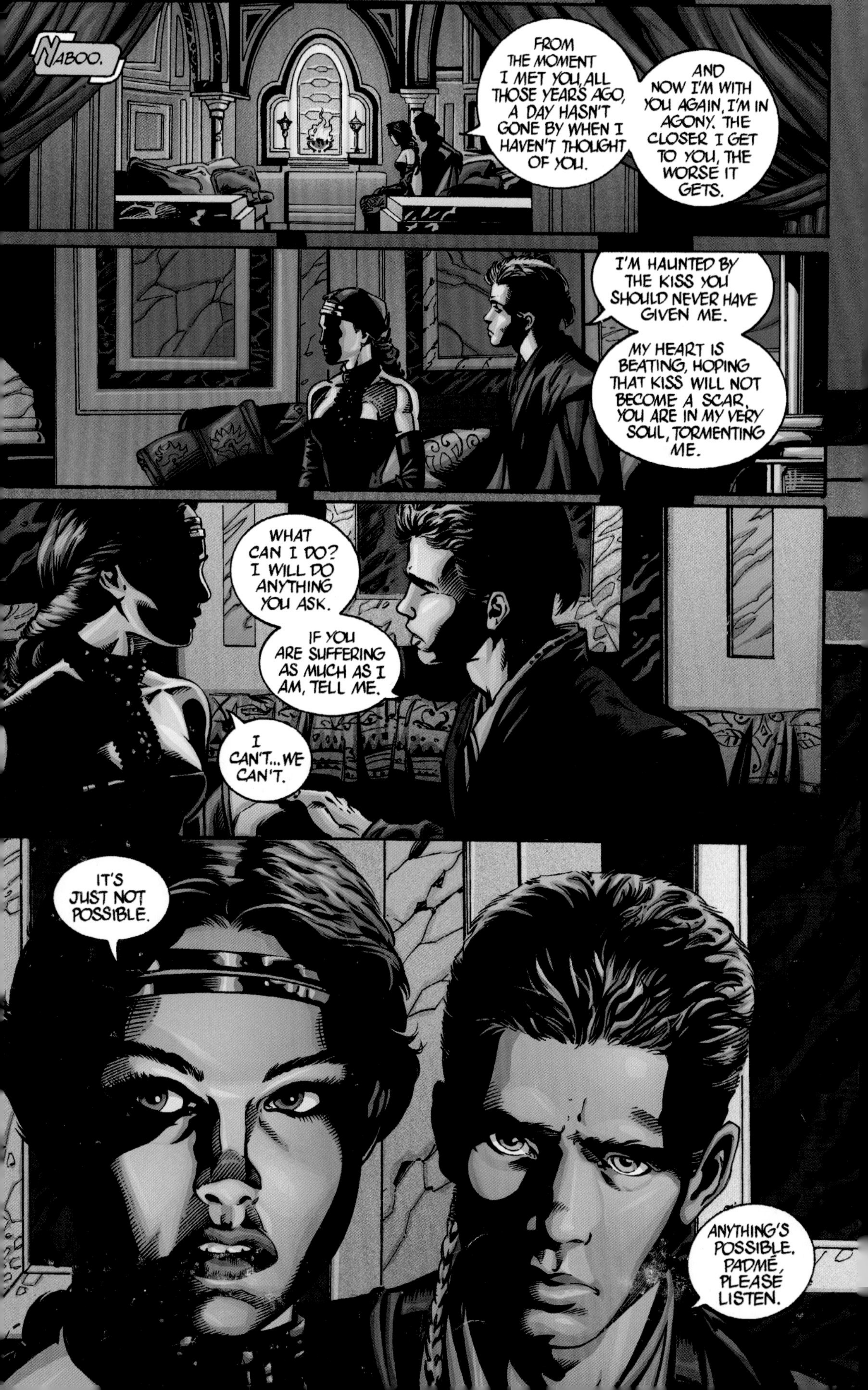
NABOO.
FROM THE MOMENT I MET YOU, ALL THOSE YEARS AGO, A DAY HASN'T GONE BY WHEN I HAVEN'T THOUGHT OF YOU.
AND NOW I'M WITH YOU AGAIN, I'M IN AGONY. THE CLOSER I GET TO YOU, THE WORSE IT GETS.
I'M HAUNTED BY THE KISS YOU SHOULD NEVER HAVE GIVEN ME.
MY HEART IS BEATING, HOPING THAT KISS WILL NOT BECOME A SCAR. YOU ARE IN MY VERY SOUL, TORMENTING ME.
WHAT CAN I DO? I WILL DO ANYTHING YOU ASK.
IF YOU ARE SUFFERING AS MUCH AS I AM, TELL ME.
I CAN'T... WE CAN'T.
IT'S JUST NOT POSSIBLE.
ANYTHING'S POSSIBLE. PADMÉ, PLEASE LISTEN.

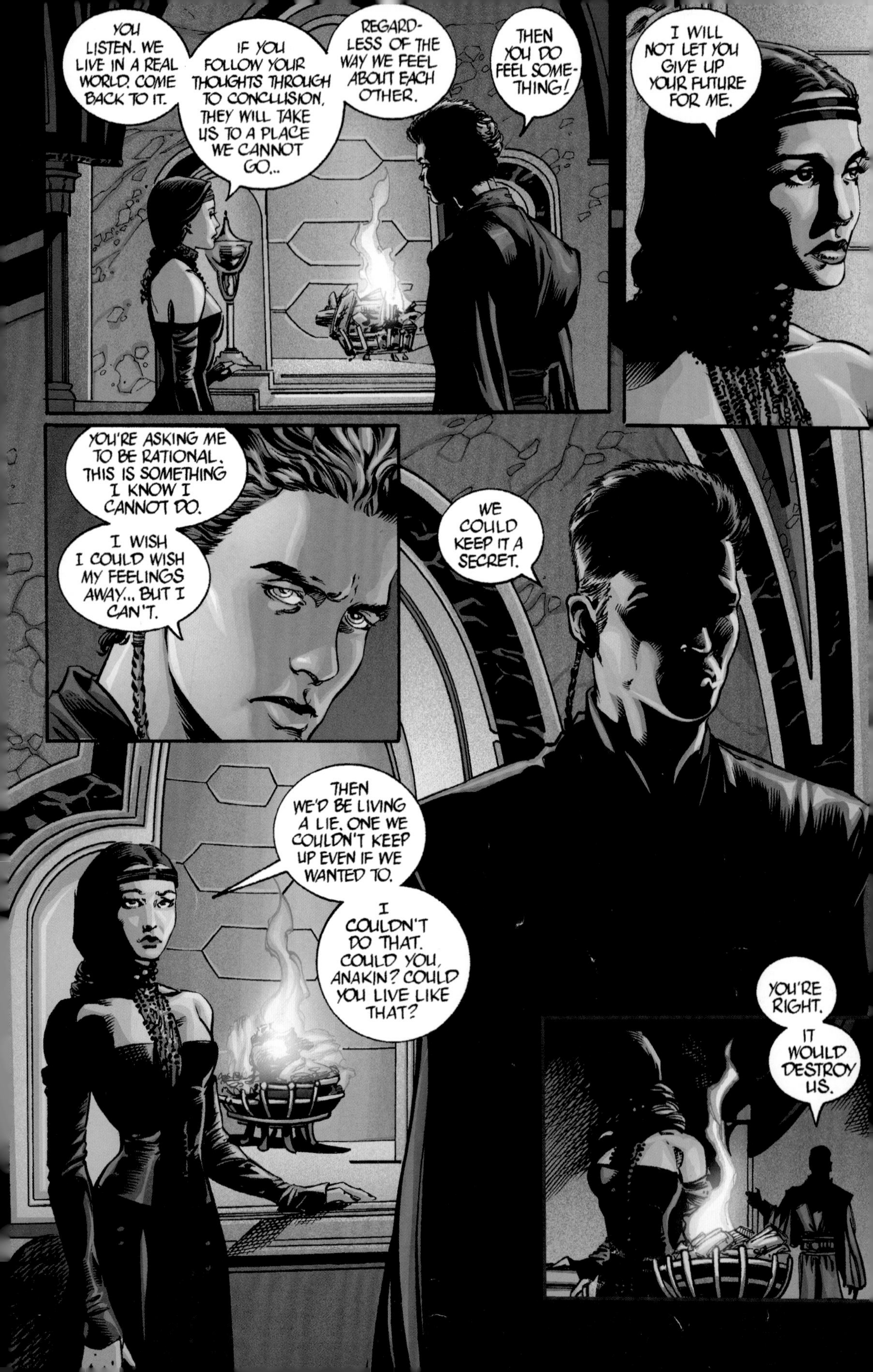
YOU LISTEN. WE LIVE IN A REAL WORLD. COME BACK TO IT.
IF YOU FOLLOW YOUR THOUGHTS THROUGH TO CONCLUSION, THEY WILL TAKE US TO A PLACE WE CANNOT GO...
REGARDLESS OF THE WAY WE FEEL ABOUT EACH OTHER.
THEN YOU DO FEEL SOMETHING!
I WILL NOT LET YOU GIVE UP YOUR FUTURE FOR ME.
YOU'RE ASKING ME TO BE RATIONAL. THIS IS SOMETHING I KNOW I CANNOT DO.
I WISH I COULD WISH MY FEELINGS AWAY... BUT I CAN'T.
WE COULD KEEP IT A SECRET.
THEN WE'D BE LIVING A LIE. ONE WE COULDN'T KEEP UP EVEN IF WE WANTED TO.
I COULDN'T DO THAT. COULD YOU, ANAKIN? COULD YOU LIVE LIKE THAT?
YOU'RE RIGHT.
IT WOULD DESTROY US.

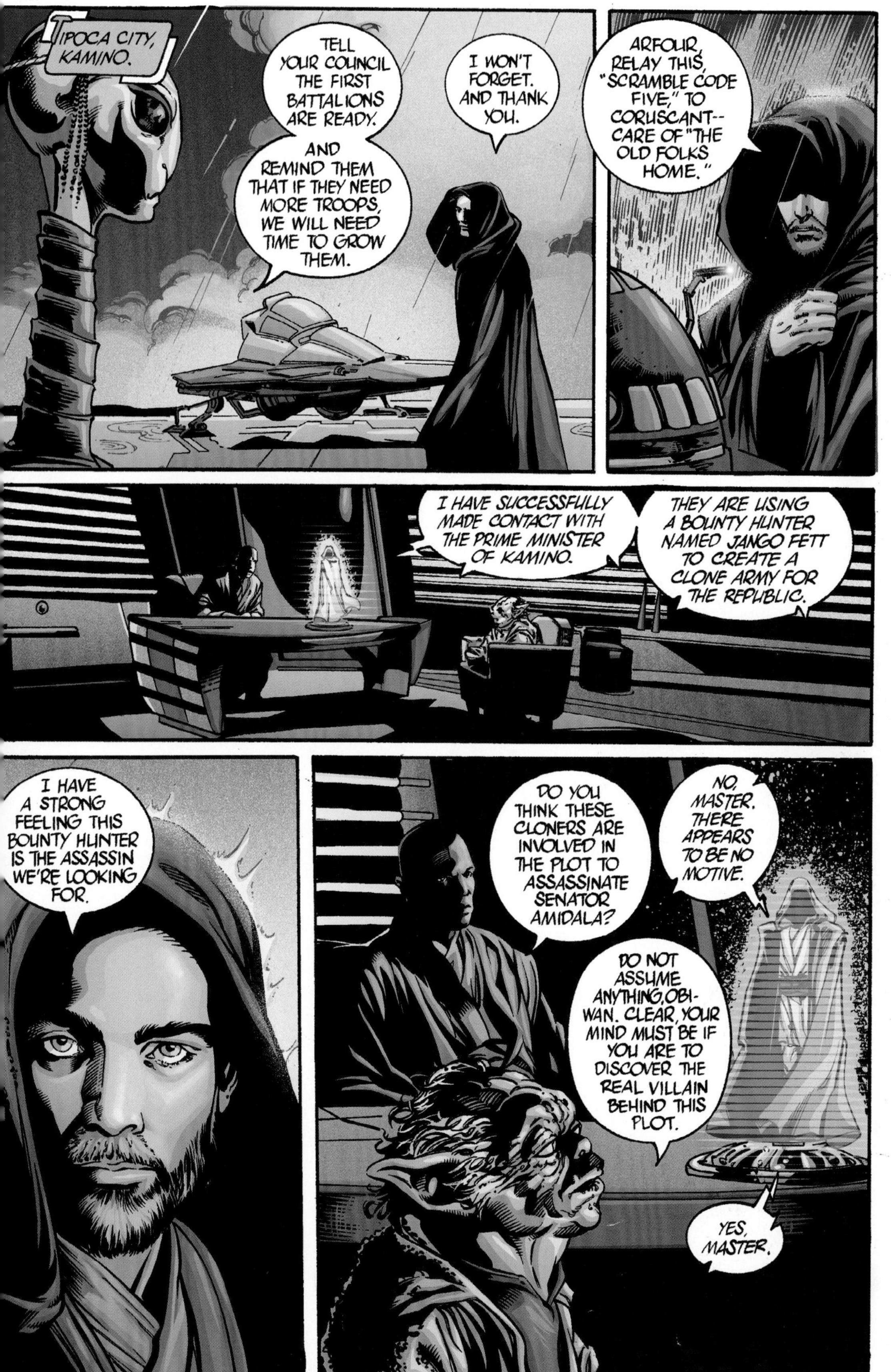
TIPOCA CITY, KAMINO.
TELL YOUR COUNCIL THE FIRST BATTALIONS ARE READY.
AND REMIND THEM THAT IF THEY NEED MORE TROOPS, WE WILL NEED TIME TO GROW THEM.
I WON'T FORGET. AND THANK YOU.
ARFOUR, RELAY THIS, "SCRAMBLE CODE FIVE," TO CORUSCANT-- CARE OF "THE OLD FOLKS HOME."
I HAVE SUCCESSFULLY MADE CONTACT WITH THE PRIME MINISTER OF KAMINO.
THEY ARE USING A BOUNTY HUNTER NAMED JANGO FETT TO CREATE A CLONE ARMY FOR THE REPUBLIC.
I HAVE A STRONG FEELING THIS BOUNTY HUNTER IS THE ASSASSIN WE'RE LOOKING FOR.
DO YOU THINK THESE CLONERS ARE INVOLVED IN THE PLOT TO ASSASSINATE SENATOR AMIDALA?
NO, MASTER. THERE APPEARS TO BE NO MOTIVE.
DO NOT ASSUME ANYTHING, OBI-WAN. CLEAR, YOUR MIND MUST BE IF YOU ARE TO DISCOVER THE REAL VILLAIN BEHIND THIS PLOT.
YES, MASTER.

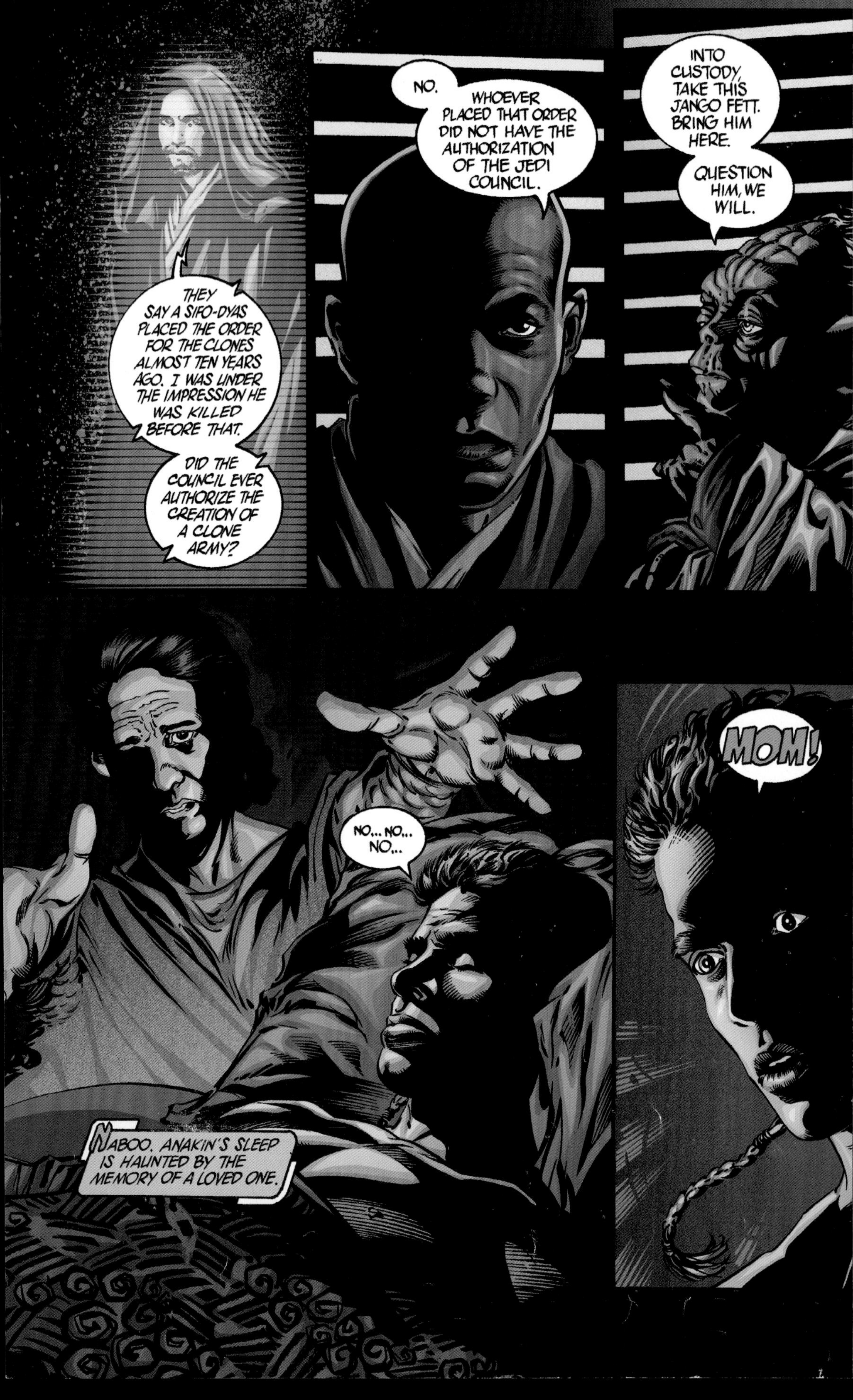
THEY SAY A SIFO-DYAS PLACED THE ORDER FOR THE CLONES ALMOST TEN YEARS AGO. I WAS UNDER THE IMPRESSION HE WAS KILLED BEFORE THAT.
DID THE COUNCIL EVER AUTHORIZE THE CREATION OF A CLONE ARMY?
NO.
WHOEVER PLACED THAT ORDER DID NOT HAVE THE AUTHORIZATION OF THE JEDI COUNCIL.
INTO CUSTODY, TAKE THIS JANGO FETT. BRING HIM HERE.
QUESTION HIM, WE WILL.
NABOO. ANAKIN'S SLEEP IS HAUNTED BY THE MEMORY OF A LOVED ONE.
NO... NO... NO...
MOM!

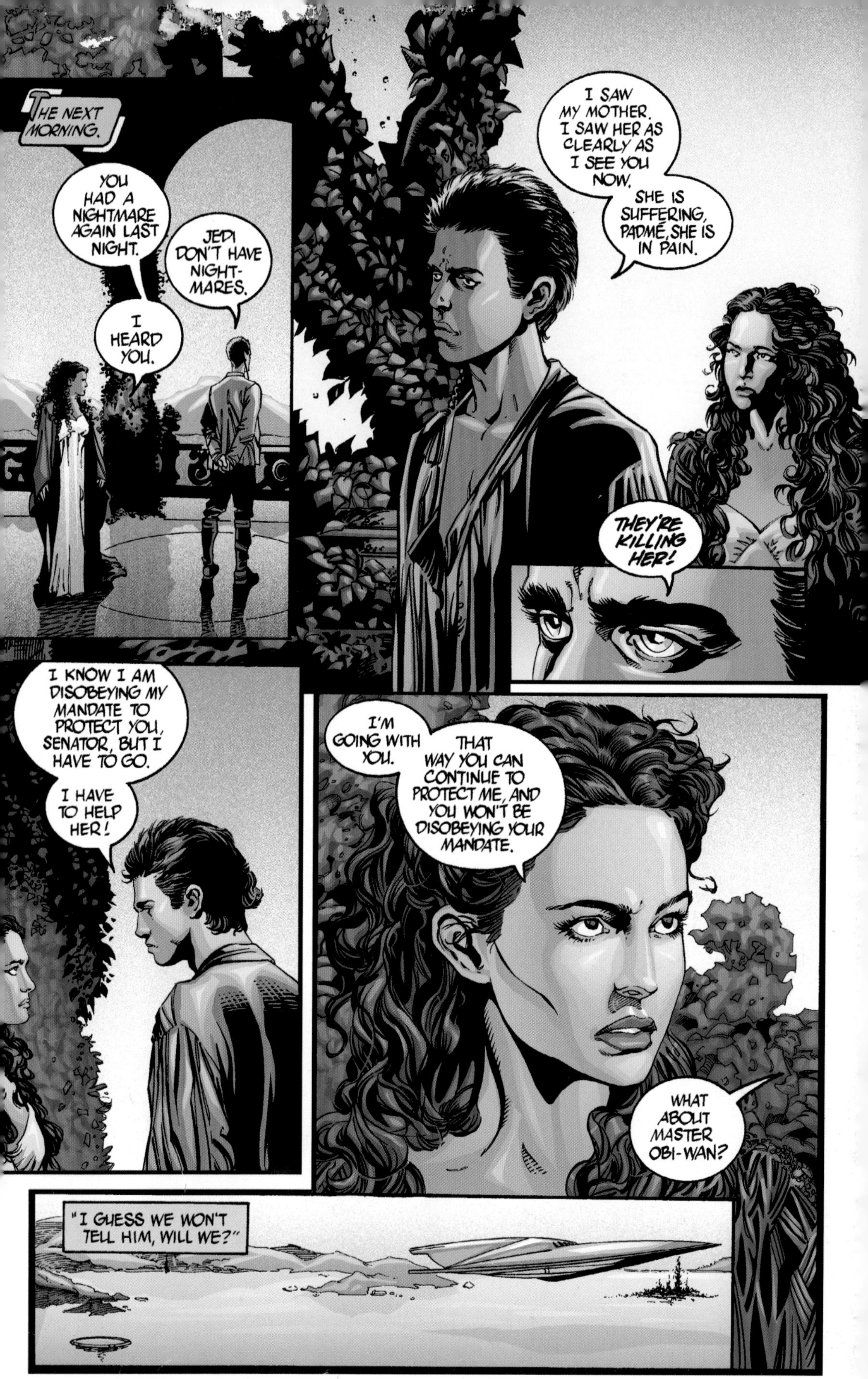
THE NEXT MORNING.
YOU HAD A NIGHTMARE AGAIN LAST NIGHT.
JEDI DON'T HAVE NIGHT-MARES.
I HEARD YOU.
I SAW MY MOTHER. I SAW HER AS CLEARLY AS I SEE YOU NOW.
SHE IS SUFFERING, PADMÉ, SHE IS IN PAIN.
THEY'RE KILLING HER!
I KNOW I AM DISOBEYING MY MANDATE TO PROTECT YOU, SENATOR, BUT I HAVE TO GO.
I HAVE TO HELP HER!
I'M GOING WITH YOU.
THAT WAY YOU CAN CONTINUE TO PROTECT ME, AND YOU WON'T BE DISOBEYING YOUR MANDATE.
WHAT ABOUT MASTER OBI-WAN?
"I GUESS WE WON'T TELL HIM, WILL WE?"

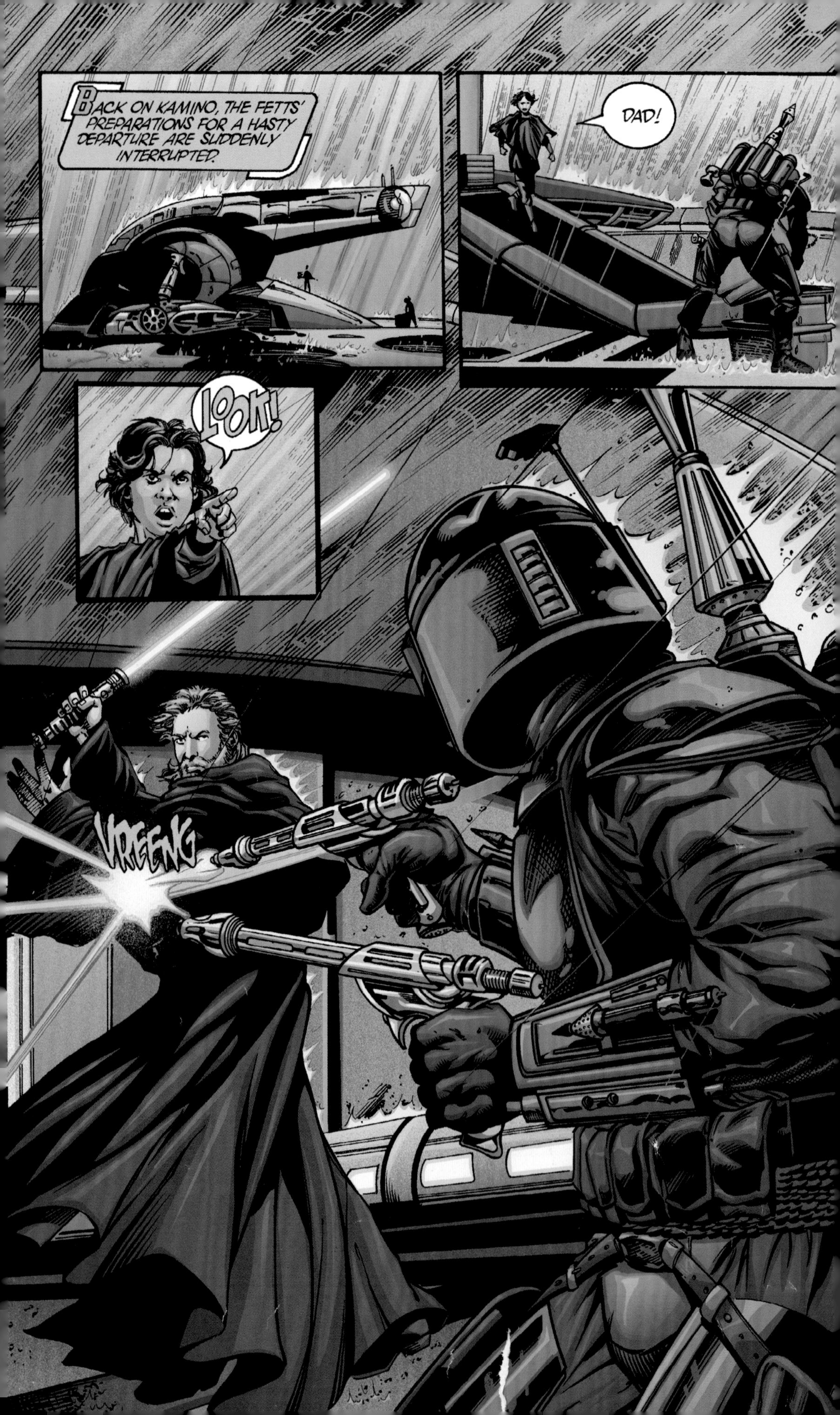
BACK ON KAMINO, THE FETTS' PREPARATIONS FOR A HASTY DEPARTURE ARE SUDDENLY INTERRUPTED.
DAD!
LOOK!
VREENG

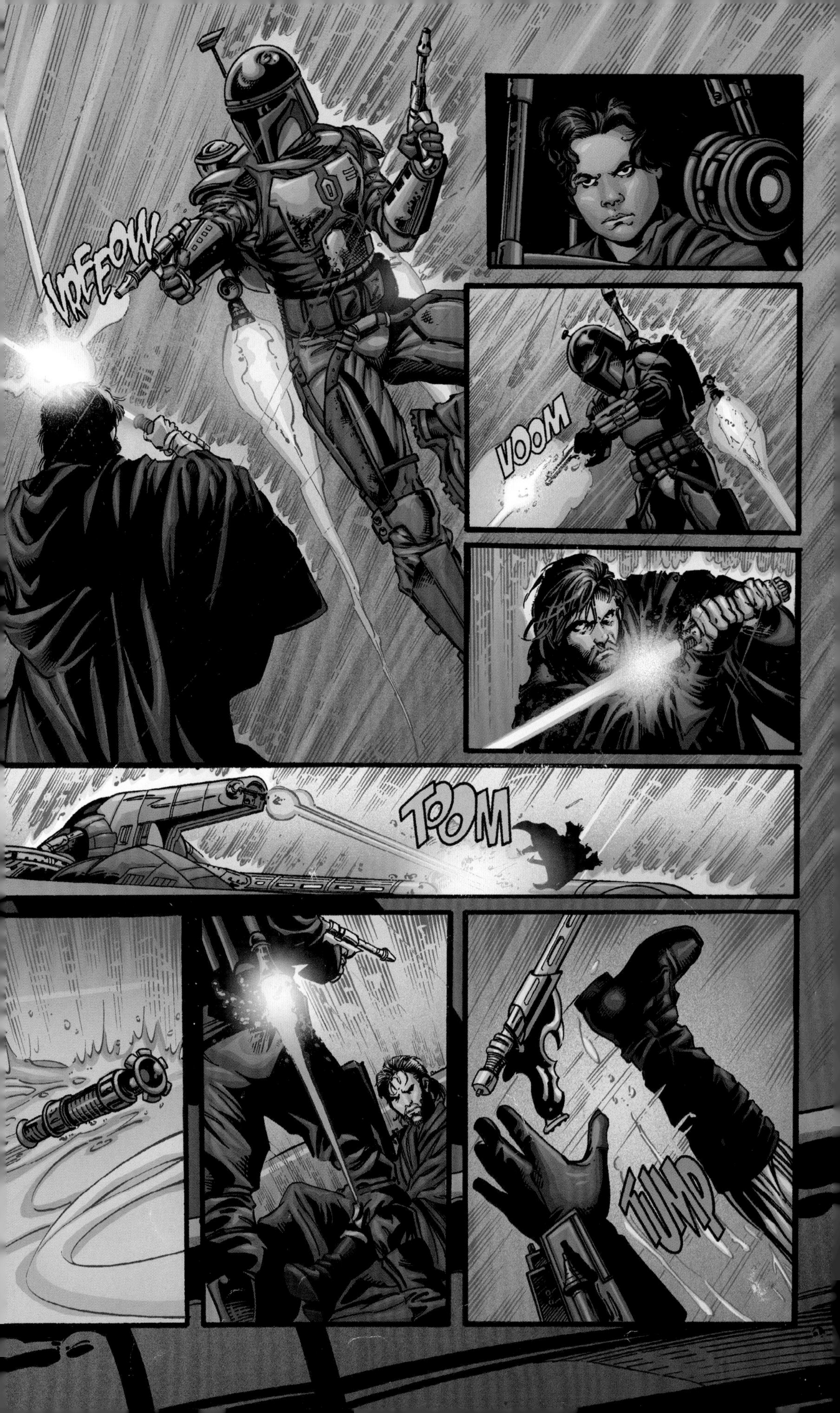
VREEOW
VOOM
TOOM

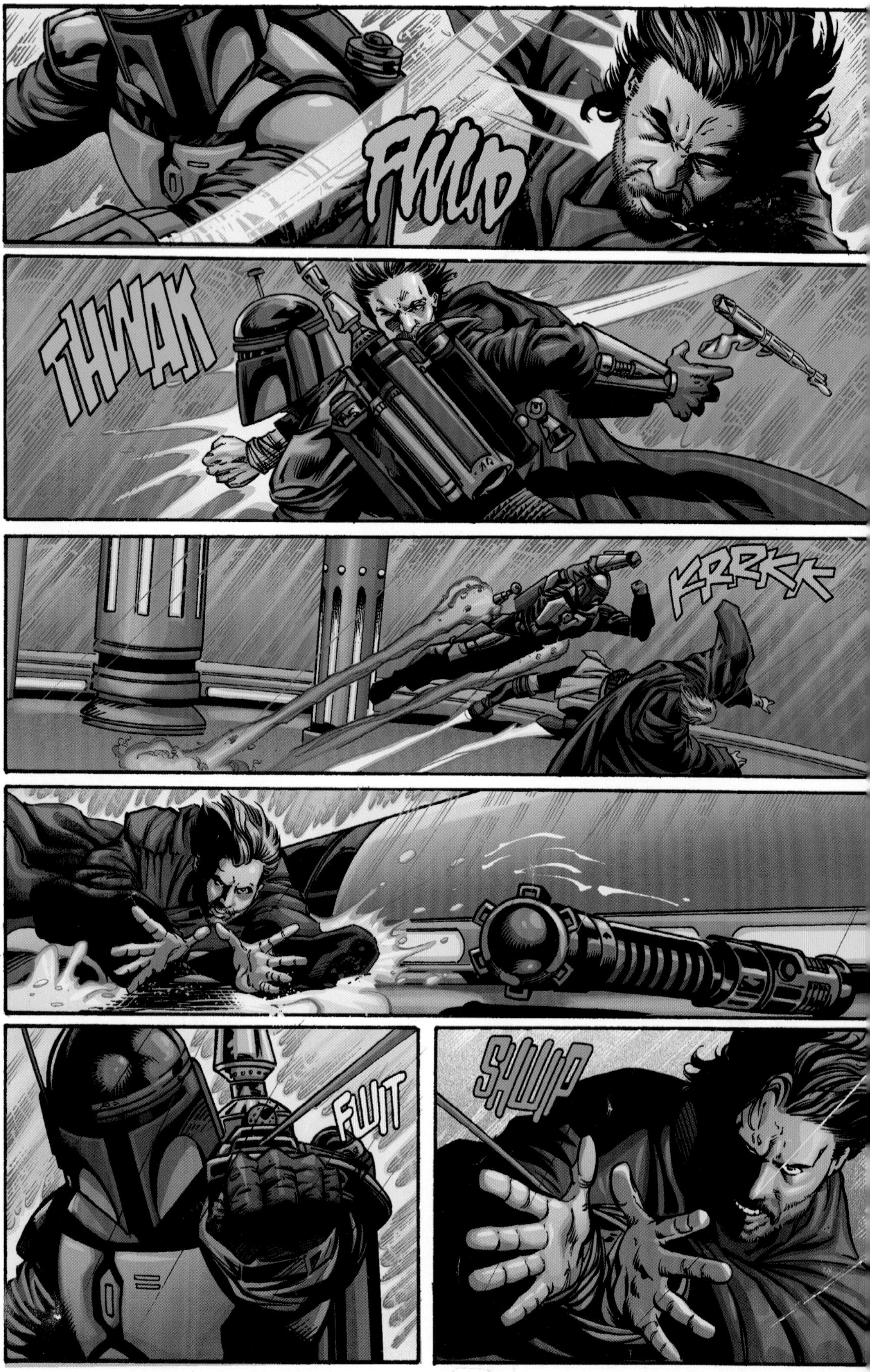
FWUD
THWAK
KRRKK
FWIT
SHWIP

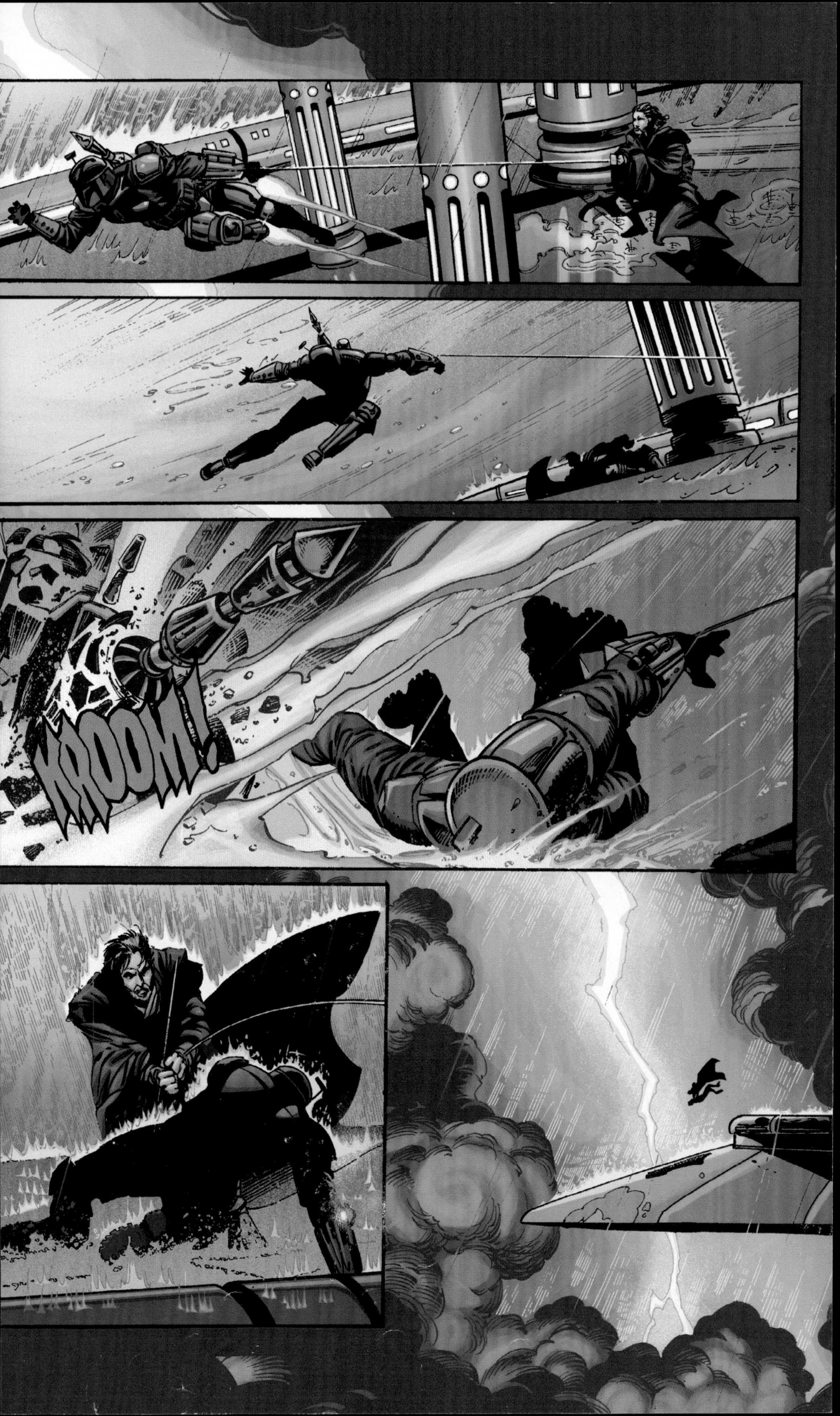
KROOM!

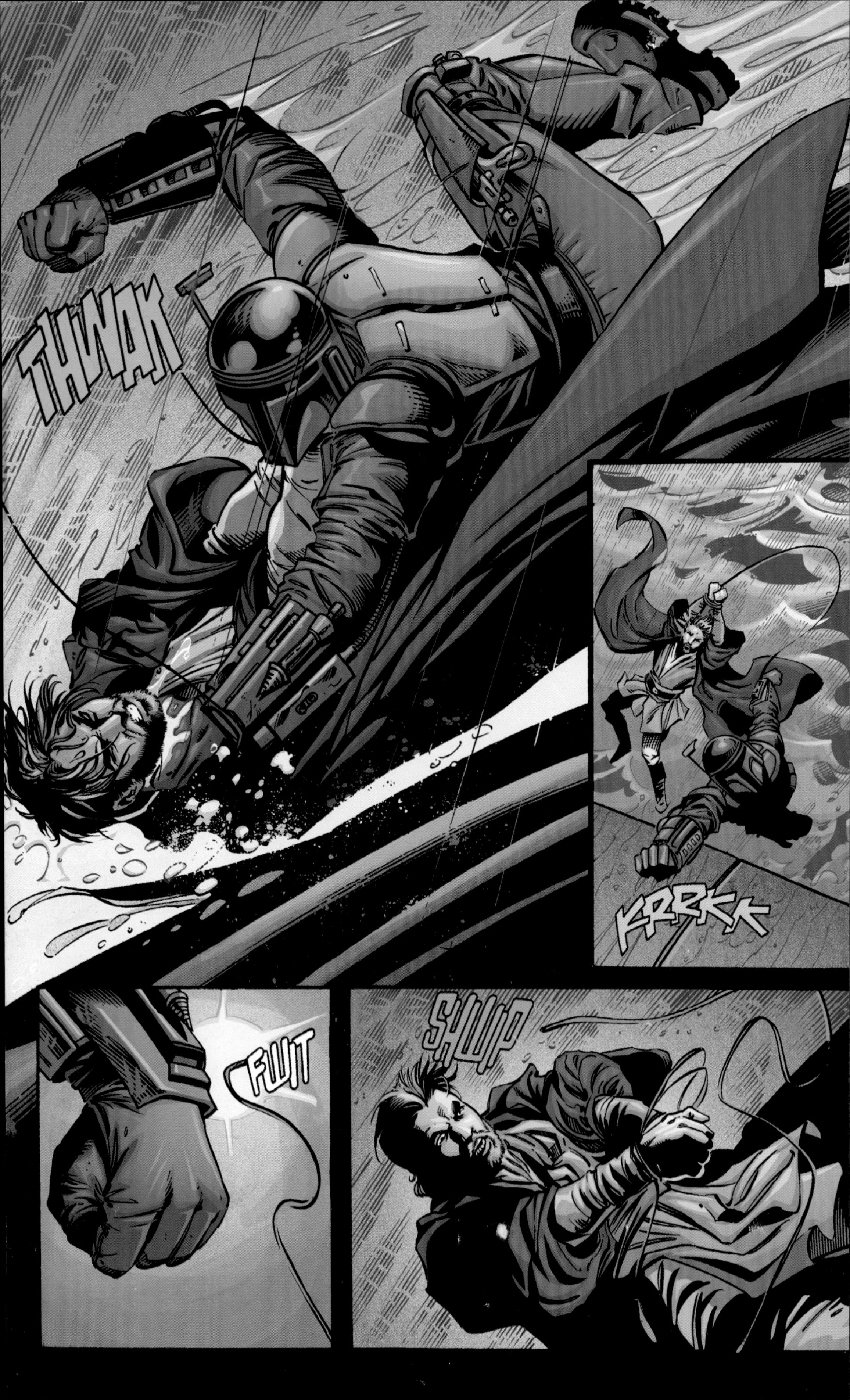
THWAK
KRRKK
FWIT
SHWIP

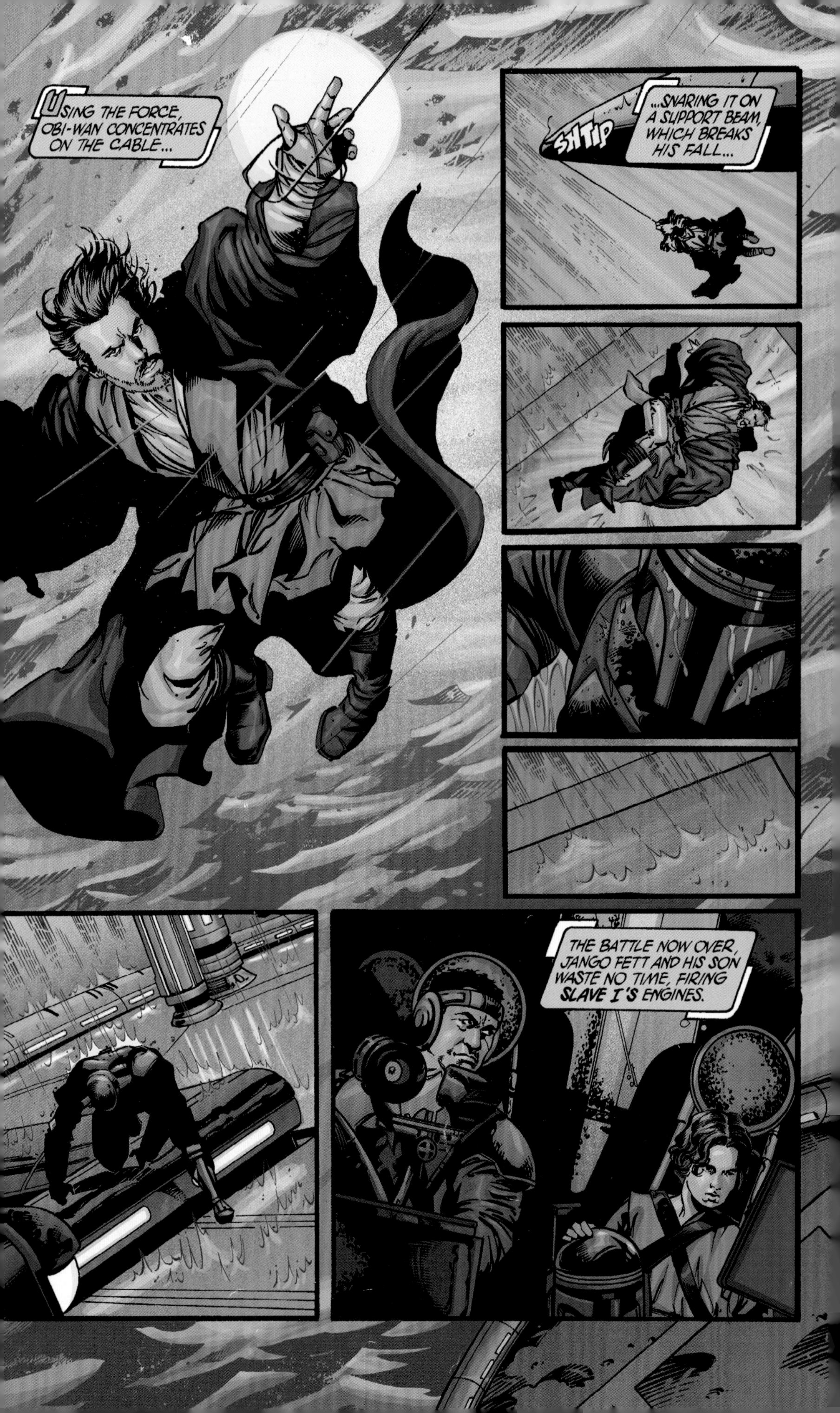
USING THE FORCE, OBI-WAN CONCENTRATES ON THE CABLE...
...SNARING IT ON A SUPPORT BEAM, WHICH BREAKS HIS FALL...
SHTIP
THE BATTLE NOW OVER, JANGO FETT AND HIS SON WASTE NO TIME, FIRING SLAVE I'S ENGINES.

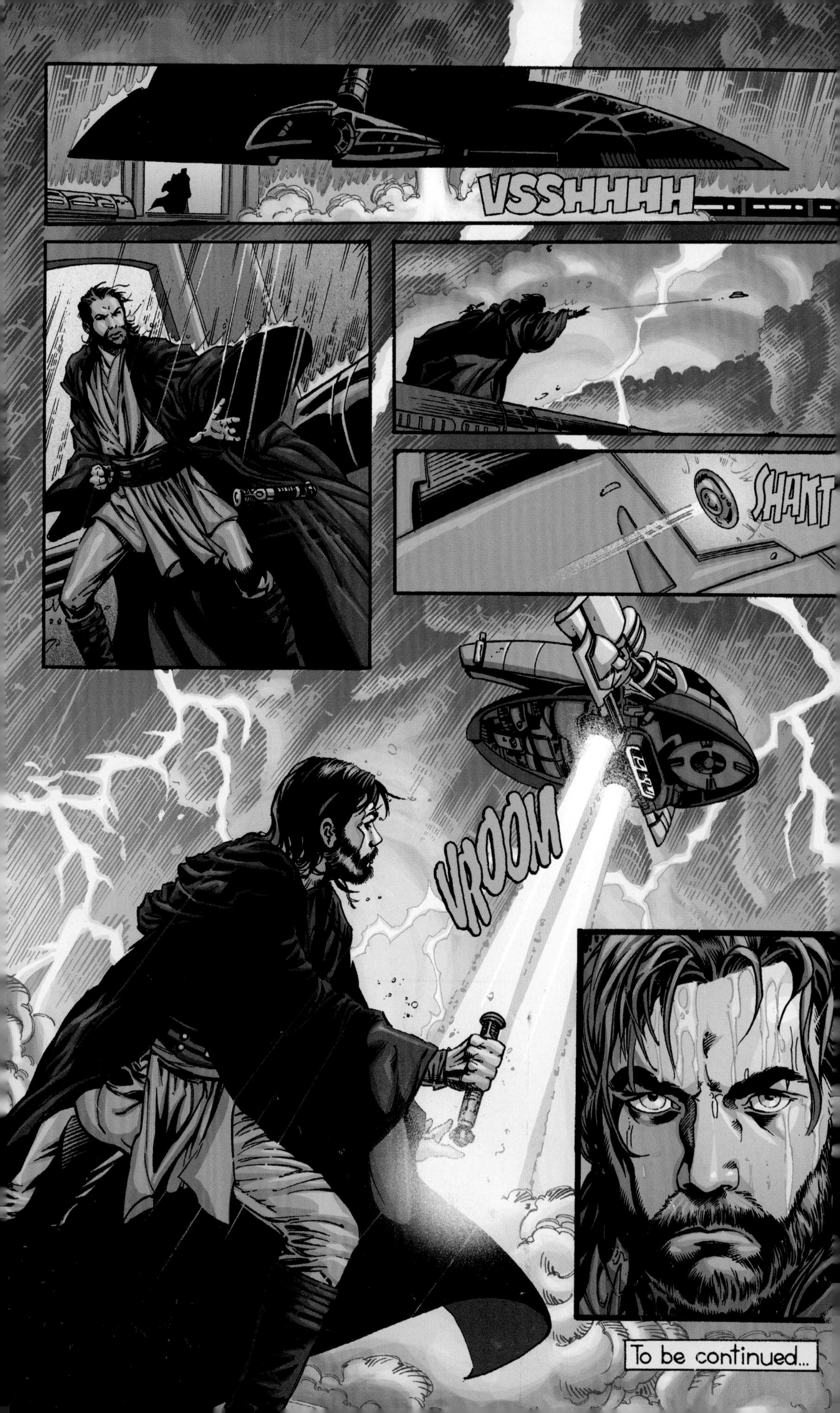
VSSHHHH
SHAKT
VROOM
To be continued...

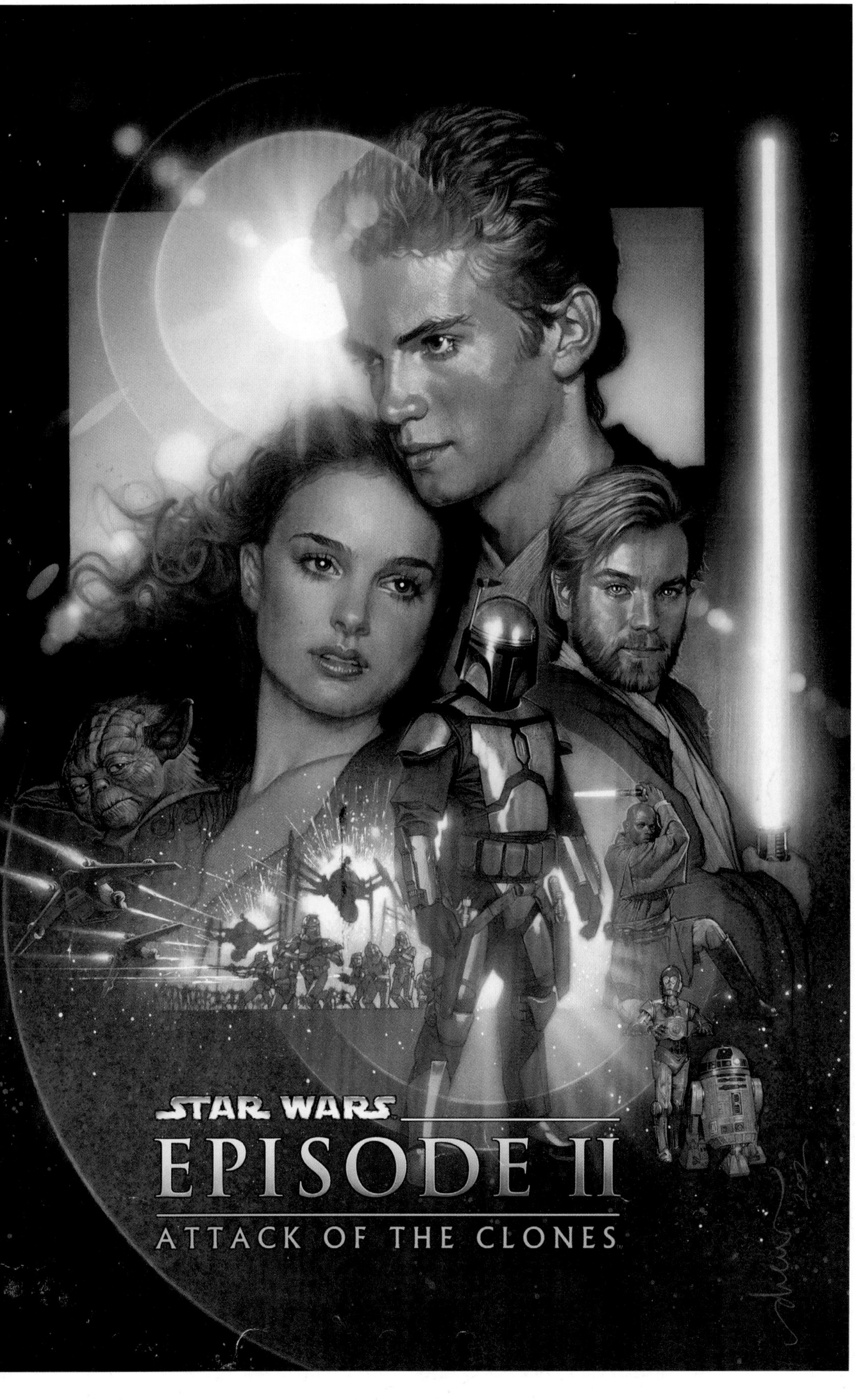
STAR WARS
EPISODE II
ATTACK OF THE CLONES

ART BY **DREW STRUZAN**

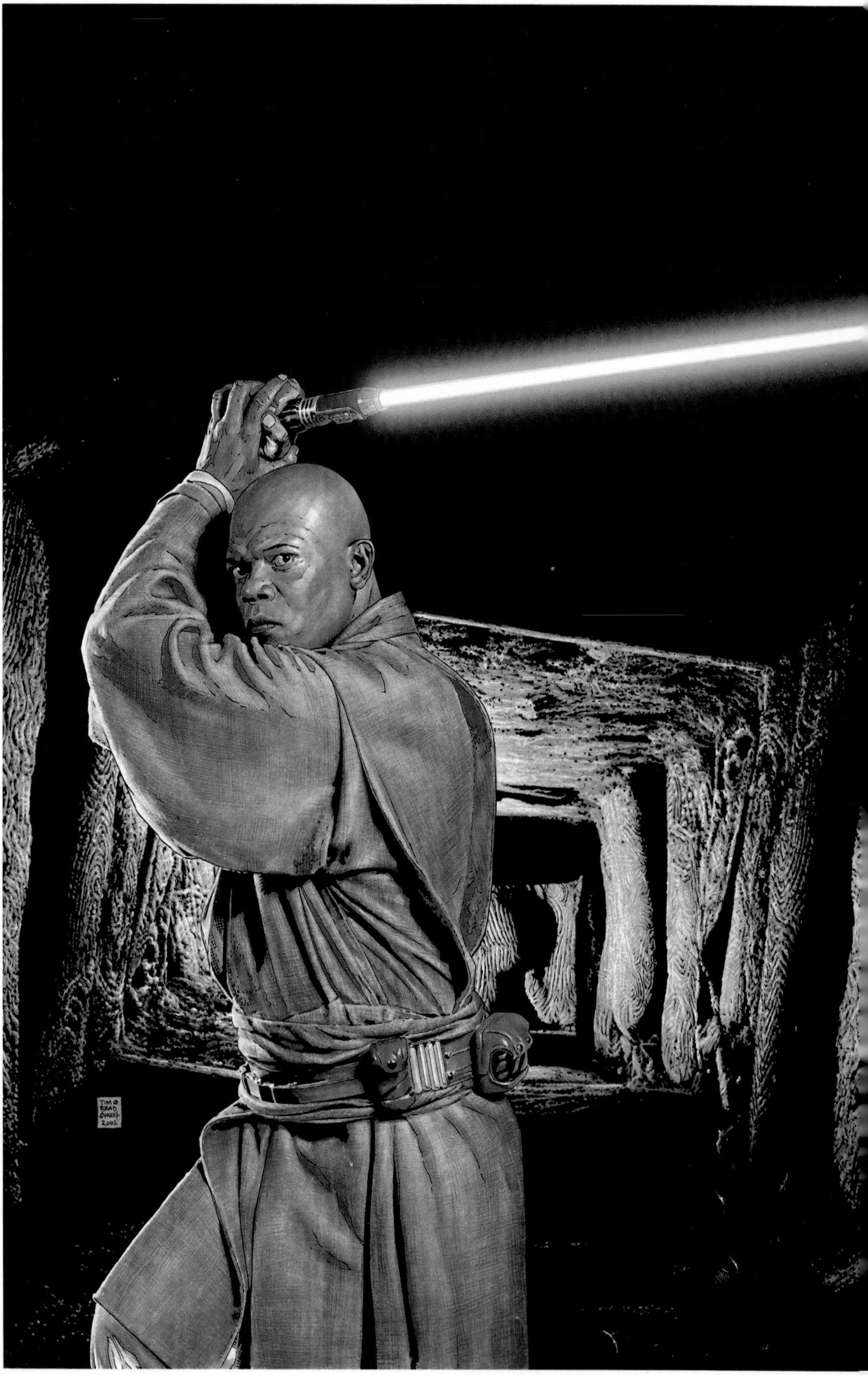

ART BY **TIM BRADSTREET**